Doctor Who — The Aztecs

DOCTOR WHO
THE AZTECS

Based on the BBC television serial by John Lucarotti by arrangement with the British Broadcasting Corporation

---

Number 88 in the
Doctor Who Library

A TARGET BOOK
published by
the Paperback Division of
W. H. ALLEN & CO. PLC

A Target Book
Published in 1984
By the Paperback Division of
W. H. Allen & Co. PLC
44 Hill Street, London W1X 8LB

First published in Great Britain by
W. H. Allen & Co. PLC 1984

Phototypeset by Sunrise Setting, Torquay, Devon
Printed and bound in Great Britain by
Anchor Brendon Ltd, Tiptree, Essex

ISBN 0 426 19588 4

CONTENTS

1

Coiled Serpent

'The TARDIS has materialised,' the Doctor announced authoritatively.

'Where?' asked Susan, the Doctor's fifteen-year-old granddaughter.

The Doctor moved around the central control deck of the spacecraft to the digital time/place orientation print-out and pressed the appropriate button. Nothing happened.

'Well?' Susan arched her eyebrows.

'Chesterton, hand me a screwdriver,' the Doctor said testily.

Ian took one from the tool-kit, and gave it to the Doctor, remarking that with any luck they were on Earth during the 1980s in an aerospace factory where the TARDIS could be thoroughly overhauled. The Doctor was not amused and began furiously unscrewing the front panel of the print-out.

'We could always stick our heads outside the door and look,' Barbara Wright suggested.

'And be devoured by a dinosaur, or dictated to by a Dalek, perhaps?' Ian added.

'Let's check the atmosphere,' Susan said.

'Good idea.' Ian turned to the Doctor. 'May I?'

The only reply was a grunt which Ian took to mean 'yes', so he switched on the atmospheric sensor. A display screen gave a breakdown of the gases ouside. Ian studied it for a moment and then said that it appeared they were on Earth, but the air was stale.

'Stale?' Susan echoed.

'Breathable but musty.'

'Then we can take a peek,' said Barbara. 'Coming with me?' she asked Susan.

When Susan asked the Doctor if she could go, he waved one hand rather vaguely at her and told Ian to help him to remove the panel. When it was off, the Doctor began poking at the electronics with his screw-driver, making the 28-year-old scientist wince with despair.

Cautiously Susan and Barbara opened the door and peered out. Apart from the light inside the TARDIS, they were in total darkness.

'Where do you think we are?' Susan whispered.

Barbara shook her head, but as the light from the TARDIS diffused and their eyes became accustomed to the gloom, they stepped outside and looked around.

They were in a large tomb, and in the centre was a raised stone slab on which lay a superbly cloaked skel-eton with a magnificent gold mask covering the skull. On the floor around the slab were earthen bowls and jugs, as well as ornaments, statuettes, bracelets, ear-rings and brooches, all of them made of jade. But it was the cloak, geometrically woven with silver and golden threads, and the superb mask that fascinated Barbara.

'Look at that, Susan,' she murmured.

'I am.' Susan shuddered with a sense of foreboding, anticipating the evil to come.

'It's an Aztec mask of Quetzecoatl, the Sun God, who

was driven into exile by Huitzilipochtli, the God of Darkness,' Barbara looked down at the skeleton again. 'He must have been a High Priest.' Beside one skeletal hand was an oblong rod of carved jade with six beaded threads of silver, each about six inches long, attached to one end. Barbara picked it up and smiled. 'Do you know what this was?'

'No.'

'His personal fly-swatter'.

Susan giggled. Since the Aztecs were Mexicans, the TARDIS must definitely be on Earth. 'But what year is it?' she asked.

'I can tell you when he died.' Barbara pointed to the objects strewn on the floor. 'About 1430. These things all come from the Aztecs' early period.' She picked up a gold bracelet shaped like a coiled snake that lay on the slab above the mask and turned it over in her hands. 'This indicates that after he died he was revered as a god.'

'You really know your subject,' Susan exclaimed. Barbara smiled and admitted that when she was at university she had been particularly interested in the Aztec Indians and their civilisation.

'What little I know about them doesn't make me feel very well disposed towards them,' Susan replied with a grimace. 'They used to cut out people's hearts while they were still alive, didn't they?'

Barbara picked up the razor-sharp knife hewn from stone which lay at the skeleton's feet. 'They did it with this,' she said. 'It's called an obsidian knife. But there was another side to their nature – a highly civilised one.'

'The Spanish didn't think so when they came here.'

'Fernando Cortez and his *conquistadores* saw only wealth for themselves and barbarous acts of savagery by the Aztecs,' Barbara replied. 'That was the tragedy of the race: their civilisation was completely destroyed, the good as well as the bad.' Barbara put down the knife and picked up the bracelet again.

'The Spanish landed in the early 1500s, didn't they?' Susan asked.

'1519, to be exact.' Still holding the bracelet Barbara pointed to the wall behind the head of the slab. A coloured fresco depicted an eagle clutching a coiled snake in its claws, surrounded by warriors in loin-cloths, cloaks, plumed head-dresses and sandals, who held shields, spears and short swords slung from their hips. From their mouths came bubbles filled with hieroglyphs. Barbara studied the fresco and, almost without realising it, slipped the bracelet onto her wrist.

'Just like cartoon strips,' Susan remarked. 'But they're all the same. What does it mean?'

'That the warriors will protect the High Priest's spirit until he rejoins his people.'

'Did the Aztecs believe in reincarnation, then?' Susan sounded surprised.

'Definitely.' Barbara moved closer to the wall. 'This painting has hardly faded at all.' She touched the mural, then quickly withdrew her hand.

'What's the matter?' Susan asked.

'It may be my imagination,' Barbara replied, 'but I think the wall moved when I touched it.'

'Let's both push it and see.'

They put their hands to the wall and began to push. The wall swung slowly outwards and upwards. Light trickled into the tomb and then flooded in as the wall rose higher and higher. Both of them blinked as their eyes adjusted to its intensity.

'This tomb is part of a temple,' Barbara whispered.

'Hadn't we better go back to the TARDIS?' Susan asked nervously.

‘No, it’s all right,’ Barbara replied, ’there’s no one here.’

‘I think I’d better fetch grandfather and Ian anyway,’ Susan said and ran back into the tomb.

Barbara left the tomb, walked to the centre of the temple and looked around. The temple itself was not large – about fifty square feet. Three sides were painted in white and blood-red, decorated with sculpted skulls and coiled snakes, and hung with elaborately woven brocade curtains. The fourth side opened onto a terrace, in the centre of which stood the sacrificial altar. Barbara shivered involuntarily as she approached the terrace to see what lay beyond it.

‘Woman!’ the man’s voice was firm and Barbara spun around to face him. He was in his mid fifties with a craggy face and long grey hair. He wore a loin-cloth, a cloak similar to the one that enveloped the skeleton in the tomb, sandals and a head-dress of multi-coloured plumed feathers. In one hand he carried a posy of flowers. ‘How came you here?’ he asked.

Barbara looked towards the entrance to the tomb in the back wall of the temple, but it had swung closed.

‘This temple is sacred to the memory of the High Priestess Yetaxa,’ the man said. ‘You trespass, and you shall be punished for it. Warriors, guardians of Yetaxa’s tomb,’ he called out. Four young Aztecs, who Barbara thought bore an uncanny resemblance to those on the mural, emerged from behind one of the curtains. ‘Seize her.’ They advanced towards Barbara who backed away to the closed entrance. It was only when she reached it with her arms outspread that the man saw the coiled-snake bracelet on her wrist.

‘Wait, warriors!’ he cried out with an expression of incredulity on his face. ‘Wait!’

The Doctor and Ian had just finished replacing the front panel when Susan burst into the TARDIS and told them excitedly where they were. The Doctor pressed the digital time-orientation button and the number 1507 lit up.

'Cortez isn't due for another twelve years,' the Doctor observed. 'But the Aztecs have some rather gruesome habits, and the sooner we collect Barbara and move on, the better.' The three of them went out into the tomb.

'The wall's closed,' Susan exclaimed.

'Which wall?' Ian asked.

'The one with the mural,' Susan replied.

'I can't see anything,' the Doctor complained, and went back into the TARDIS to fetch his pencil-torch. When he came out again he switched it on, but the beam of light was too narrow.

'I still can't see anything,' he grumbled.

'Give me your hand, grandfather,' Susan said and led him past the raised slab.

'What's that?' the Doctor asked.

'According to Barbara, he was a High Priest now revered as a god,' Susan replied.

The Doctor snorted.

'We push it up,' Susan explained when they reached the wall, and a few seconds later they were standing in the temple.

'Barbara's not here,' Ian said.

'She was when I came to fetch you,' replied Susan defensively.

Ian called out Barbara's name. 'There's no sign of her now,' he said, 'unless she's out on that terrace.' He walked to the sacrificial altar and glanced down either side of the terrace. 'She's not out here.' Then he looked down. 'Good Lord, Doctor, come and see this,' he exclaimed.

Both the Doctor and Susan went to Ian's side. As they passed the altar the Doctor muttered that they had better find Barbara soon as he didn't fancy being carved up on it by some Aztec High Priest of Sacrifice.

'Just look at the city,' said Ian. The temple was on the top of a pyramid and the city lay two hundred and fifty feet below them, patterned like a chessboard, with broad avenues between the squares of houses. There were gardens, irrigation aqueducts, and several markets.

'The Aztecs knew how to build as well as kill,' the Doctor observed drily. 'We must find Barbara and leave.' He looked back into the temple and saw the wall sliding back into place. 'The wall, Chesterton! Quick! The wall!' he cried, and Ian raced across the temple in a vain attempt to reach the wall before it shut them out. The Doctor and Susan hurried after him.

'I was too late. There was nothing to grip on to.' Ian felt ashamed at his failure.

Susan looked perplexed. 'But it must open somehow, Ian.'

'It does, child,' the Doctor said with a shrug, 'you push it from the other side. Tombs like these were designed to stop grave-robbers, not help them.'

'But how shall we return to the TARDIS?'

'That, my dear, is a very good question.'

Ian cleared his throat. 'Doctor, we've company,' he murmured.

The man whom Barbara had met and the four Aztec warriors were standing by one of the brocade curtains. The man raised in salute a hand which held a posy of flowers.

'Autloc, High Priest of Knowledge, most humbly greets the servants of Yetaxa,' he said, while the four warriors bowed.

The Doctor glanced at Ian. 'The servants of what?' he asked.

Ian shook his head and looked at the High Priest. 'Where is Barbara?'

'Of whom do you speak?'

'The young woman who was here a few moments ago.'

The High Priest smiled at them. 'In due course you will meet Yetaxa again. But first, grant us our courtesies. Be assured that we harbour no evil towards you in our hearts. Indeed, we honour you.'

The Doctor looked at Autloc for a moment. 'What did you say your name was?' He sounded suspicious.

'Autloc.'

'And you're the High Priest of Knowledge.'

'I serve as such.'

'You know where we came from?' the Doctor persisted.

'Yetaxa's tomb.'

'How does one enter it from the temple?'

'One cannot. It is sealed.' Autloc gestured towards the four warriors. 'Go now with these attendants and soon you will see the coiled serpent of Yetaxa again.'

The Doctor scratched his head. 'I don't know what he's talking about,' he said as they crossed the temple to where a warrior held aside one of the curtains.

'Barbara, I think,' Susan hissed, 'I'll explain when we're alone.'

Just before they reached the drawn curtain, the deformed figure of a powerfully built man limped into the temple from the terrace. He was younger than Autloc and far less elaborately dressed. He wore a priest's loose-fitting robe which at first glance appeared to be caked in mud, but a second look told Susan it was dried blood. The plumes on his head-dress were splattered with it and his long hair was matted. He had a hard, thin, almost lipless mouth. But it was his eyes that commanded attention – they were jet black, piercing and totally fanatical. He stared at the Doctor, at Susan and at Ian, then bowed curtly to them and limped to the back of the temple where Autloc stood.

'You know who he is, Chesterton,' the Doctor said as they were escorted from the temple.

'The local butcher, by the look of him,' Ian replied.

'Exactly.'

Autloc waited until they had gone before he spoke.

'You have seen her, Tlotoxl?' he asked.

'A vision is with us, Autloc,' Tlotoxl replied and, turning away, he limped back to the sacrificial altar. He looked up at the sky. 'When does it rain?'

Autloc came half-way along the length of the temple and looked with distaste at Tlotoxl's back. 'This day when the sun's fire first touches the horizon to the west,' he replied.

'At that moment we will present her to the people. A vision shall stand before them, and I, in supplication to Tlaloc, the Rain God,' Tlotoxl stretched out his left hand over the altar, 'I shall offer human blood. And the rain will come. No more talk of Tlaloc being angered by us and bringing drought to the land. There will be rain,' he exulted, 'and all power shall be ours again.' Facing the altar, Tlotoxl raised both hands and shook his clenched fists to the heavens.

'I tell you, High Priest of Sacrifice, there will be rain,' Autloc spoke gently and hesitated before continuing, '– with or without human blood.'

Tlotoxl spun around, his eyes ablaze. 'Does the High Priest of Knowledge serve only Quetzecoatl, the banished God, and not Huitzilipochtli who has made us strong?'

'I serve the same God as you.' Autloc's voice was even.

'Then, above all else, honour him. He demands blood,' Tlotoxl shouted, 'and he shall have it.'

The Doctor, Susan and Ian were in an antechamber below the temple. The walls were covered with colourful tapestries; the stone floor was carpeted; there were three couches to recline on, and a legless table laden with food and wine. Susan and Ian sat down while the Doctor paced up down.

'So you think Barbara may have been wearing the bracelet when she went into the temple, is that it, Susan?' The Doctor didn't stop to look at her.

'I know Barbara picked it up and I have a feeling she may have put it on,' Susan replied half-apologetically, 'but I can't be sure, grandfather, it was dark in the tomb.'

'If she were wearing the bracelet and came out of the tomb then that fellow Itloc –'

'Autloc,' Ian corrected him, and was ignored.

' – must associate Barbara in some way with that skeleton, Texaya.'

'Yetaxa.' It was Susan's turn to put him right.

'Very interesting,' the Doctor muttered.

'Well, they've treated us all right so far,' Susan said brightly.

The Doctor stopped in his tracks and glared at her. 'The Aztecs always showed the utmost courtesy to their intended victims,' he observed icily and continued pacing the room.

2

Yetaxa the God

The Doctor was still marching up and down muttering to himself when a warrior came into the antechamber and beckoned them to follow him up the candle-lit stairs to the temple. Once there, the warrior drew back the brocade curtain and stood to one side to let them pass. The temple had been transformed. The entire back wall, behind which was Yetaxa's tomb, had been covered with a clear sea-blue curtain filigreed in gold and silver threads with fish, sea-shells and crabs, symbols of Tlaloc, the God of Water. In front of the curtain was a stone dais studded with pieces of jade, turquoise and emerald. On the dais stood a golden throne whose delicately worked trellis back was surmounted by a golden eagle with a coiled snake held in its beak. But the most remarkable transformation of all was Barbara. She was seated on the throne, dressed in a knee-length silk skirt patterned with multicoloured zig-zags. Her green lace blouse was decorated with sheaves of corn and leaves woven in gold thread. Around her waist she wore a leather belt with an emerald buckle. Her necklace was jade, as were the bracelets she wore on her left arm; on her right wrist she wore the coiled snake from Yetaxa's tomb and she held a posy of flowers. Her head-dress was a gold crown decked with brilliantly coloured plumes, and her sandals were laced with gold thread. The Doctor, Susan and Ian gaped at her in astonishment.

Barbara glanced at the warrior who stood beside the brocade curtain. 'Leave us,' she commanded.

The warrior bowed and withdrew from the temple.

'Barbara, what on earth are you doing there?' Ian's voice echoed his incredulity.

Barbara leaned her right elbow on the arm of the throne, held up her hand and shook her wrist, the posy and the snake.

'They think I'm the reincarnation of the High Priest in the tomb.'

'Because you had put on the bracelet and were caught wearing it by the High Priest of Knowledge,' the Doctor concluded for her.

'That's correct, Doctor,' said Barbara. 'Autloc knew that I had come out of Yetaxa's tomb.'

Susan looked puzzled. 'But if Yetaxa was a man,' she asked, 'how can they believe you are a reincarnation of him?'

'The form his spirit takes isn't important to them, Susan.' Barbara pointed to the bracelet. 'This is what counted.'

'Autloc called us Yetaxa's servants,' Ian said. 'Is that who they think we are – your servants?'

Barbara nodded apologetically.

'Charming!' the Doctor snorted.

Barbara turned to him. 'But it's ideal, Doctor. We can enter the tomb as soon as we like, get into the TARDIS and be on our way.'

The Doctor drily observed that although re-incarnations could come out of the tomb, human beings couldn't go into one.

'You're a god, Barbara,' Ian said with a smile. 'Find out how it opens.'

Barbara replied that she would ask, but the Doctor tut-tutted testily.

'That's the one thing you must not do.' His voice was severe. 'As Yetaxa's spirit, you'll be expected to know everything. But if you go around asking questions and the Aztecs were to decide that you're not whom they think you are,' the Doctor paused for effect, 'then we won't last long.' The Doctor sighed and walked around the throne. Susan and Ian didn't move. They all realised there was an impenetrable wall between them and the solution to their problem.

The two High Priests came into the temple and bowed to Barbara.

'Great spirit of Yetaxa,' Tlotoxl said, 'the High Priest of Sacrifice salutes you.'

The Doctor and Ian exchanged a glance.

'I acknowledge the High Priest's greeting,' Barbara replied.

Autloc approached the throne. 'For many days and many nights Tlaloc has looked away from us,' he began, but Barbara interrupted him.

'The God of Water and Vegetation?'

Autloc nodded. 'Our land withers and the people groan.'

Tlotoxl limped closer to Barbara. 'Those who serve the temple have prayed that the land may again be bountified,' he said, 'and this day we shall honour Tlaloc's name.'

'When the sun's fire touches the horizon to the west, the people will stand before the temple in obedience to our commands,' said Autloc and bowed again. 'We humbly beg you, Great Spirit, at that time, to show yourself before the people so that they may know their suffering draws to an end.'

The Doctor leant over to Ian and muttered gleefully that Barbara would appear and down would come the rain.

'How can he be so sure?' Ian asked out of the corner of his mouth.

'He's not the High Priest of Knowledge for nothing, Chesterton,' the Doctor replied.

Tlotoxl was watching them.

'I shall do as the High Priest requests,' Barbara said.

'We also entreat you, Great Spirit, to permit your handmaiden and servants to perambulate among our people,' Autloc continued.

The Doctor saw the flicker of doubt in Barbara's eyes. He stepped forward.

'Great Spirit, grant this request.' He pointed to Ian and himself. 'Thus may we be your eyes and ears and learn how best to serve all our interests.'

'The aged servant of Yetaxa speaks with wisdom,' Autloc remarked, looking at the Doctor with interest.

The Doctor bristled. Aged indeed, he thought.

Barbara pointed to Susan. 'My handmaiden remains with me.' She waved her hand at Ian and the Doctor. 'But they may do as you request.'

The High Priests bowed again to Barbara, then Autloc turned to Ian and the Doctor. 'We shall await you,' he said, and they left the temple.

Once they had disappeared behind the curtain, the Doctor rubbed his hands in delight.

'A beautiful performance, my dear,' he enthused. 'We've got exactly what we want. You and Susan here in perfect safety, Chesterton and myself out and about, trying to find a way to get back behind that wall, into the TARDIS and off.'

Ian wasn't convinced. 'It sounds all right,' he said, 'but

I don't think we should take our eyes off those two High Priests for a second.'

'Don't worry about them, Chesterton,' the Doctor replied airily, 'they'll be too busy timing their miracle.'

'What miracle?' Susan asked.

The Doctor turned to her. 'Presenting the great Spirit of Yetaxa to the people, one second before there is a flash of lightning, a clap of thunder and it buckets down.'

'I still don't see how they can be as accurate as that,' Ian said, shaking his head.

The Doctor wagged a forefinger at him. 'You mustn't underestimate the Aztecs, Chesterton. They were a very civilised, cultured people.'

'Not were – are, as far as we are concerned,' Ian interjected.

The Doctor cleared his throat. 'They know all about about astronomy and the constellations, each of which has its own minor god; their agricultural policies and practices are centuries ahead of their time; and look at the workmanship on Barbara's throne,' he pointed dramatically to it. 'A very advanced people, apart from one or two glaring shortcomings.'

'Such as cutting out people's hearts, or chucking them off the temple steps,' Susan suggested.

The Doctor dismissed her with a look. 'I was talking scientifically,' he said haughtily, 'for example, they don't know about the wheel.'

The two High Priests waited for Ian and the Doctor in the antechamber below the temple. Autloc was studying his posy of flowers whilst Tlotoxl toyed with the obsidian knife he had extracted from under his priest's robe.

'Autloc, who serves Yetaxa?' he asked suddenly.

'We do, as High Prists of the temple,' Autloc replied.

'What purpose then serve the others?'

'Yetaxa has said that the . . .'

Before Autloc had finished speaking, Tlotoxl pointed the knife at him and asked if it would not be better that one of the strangers should lead their force of arms. 'Yetaxa's young servant should enjoy this honour. A warrior favoured by the Gods.'

Autloc considered this proposal for a moment, trying to guess what Tlotoxl's ulterior motive might be. 'But Ixta is our chosen warrior,' he replied finally.

Tlotoxl limped over to Autloc's side. 'Let Ixta prove himself more worthy of command than the servant of Yetaxa,' he murmured, touching the tip of the knife with his finger.

'But were the servant to lose the contest, it would bring down Yetaxa's wrath upon us,' Autloc countered.

Tlotoxl almost smiled as he hinted that Yetaxa would ensure that no harm came to her servant, as the Gods were all-powerful.

Autloc was disquieted and tugged at a petal of a flower as he wondered again what Tlotoxl's purpose was.

The Doctor and Ian entered the antechamber.

Tlotoxl sheathed the obsidian knife. 'It has been decided the aged servant may walk abroad,' he announced, 'but you,' he said, turning to Ian, 'will train to command our armies.'

Ian and the Doctor looked anxiously at one another. Don't argue, said the look on the Doctor's face.

'The Great Spirit of Yetaxa would not deny me such an honour,' Ian replied.

Tlotoxl turned to Autloc and asked him to conduct the Doctor to the garden at the base of the temple. 'There you may sit in comfort with others of advanced years,' he added to an inwardly fuming Doctor, whom Autloc beckoned to follow him down the flights of stairs that would lead them to the ground level of the pyramid.

Then Tlotoxl pointed to the jug of wine and one of the goblets. Ian shook his head, but the High Priest picked up the jug, filled a goblet and drank the wine in a single draught. He put the goblet back on the table and wiped his mouth with the sleeve of his robe. He looked at Ian for a few seconds with his intense, dark eyes.

'Come now with me to the barracks,' he said, 'where you shall encounter Ixta.'

'Ixta? Is that someone's name?' Ian asked.

'Yes. He is your rival for command,' Tlotoxl replied and limped towards the stairs.

Considerably taken aback, Ian followed, rather wishing he had accepted the proffered glass of wine.

The Doctor was slightly out of breath when he and Autloc came out of the temple. He looked up at the pyramid towering above him and recalled Susan's remark concerning the faster way down and decided he was more than content to pant a bit. Autloc led the way to the high-walled garden behind the temple. In one wall was a wooden door which Autloc opened and let the two of them into the garden. It was enormous and beautifully laid out. The inside of the walls was trellised and covered with the rose and purple hues of bougainvillea vines. In the centre of the garden was a lake with an island of multicoloured rocks in the middle. A mosaic path encircled the lake, with small paths radiating from it to the walls, and another three concentric paths cut the garden into segments, each one a trimmed lawn with beds of flowers and shrubs. There were stone benches along the edges of the lawns where older Aztecs sat. They bowed their heads respectfully to Autloc, looked curiously at the Doctor's clothes and whispered amongst themselves.

The Doctor surveyed the scene around him. Colour abounded. 'A pleasant venue for a reflective afternoon,' he observed.

'Many years ago, after the body of the High Priest Yetaxa was sealed in the tomb, a law was introduced that all who attain their fifty-second year should pleasurably pass the remainder of their years, free from responsibility and care,' Autloc explained.

'Highly commendable, but don't they sometimes become bored?'

'Often we seek the accumulated wisdom of their years.'

'What about?'

'All manner of things. Each person here served the community in one way or another.' Autloc began pointing them out. 'He was a weaver of priestly robes; she was a woman of medicines; he, an artisan of gold and silver; she, a sculptress in obsidian stone; and that man, a leading architect in the modernisation of our city.'

The Doctor noticed a grey-haired, pleasant-faced, plumpish woman in her mid fifties who was using a knife to prune a rose bush. 'That lady was, and still is, a gardener, I take it?' the Doctor asked.

Autloc laughed. 'Cameca's advice, of all those here, is the most sought after. She sold vegetables in the market-place but her eyes were everywhere, missing nothing. You will find in her a companion of great wit and interest,' Autloc added.

'What did you say she was called? Names have never been my forte.'

'Cameca,' Autloc replied and begged the Doctor's permission to return to the temple. The Doctor acquiesced and Autloc strode away.

'Cameca, yes,' the Doctor muttered to himself. He had already noticed her glancing furtively at him. He wandered along the path, holding a lapel of his jacket, and stopped beside her. Cameca concentrated on her pruning.

'Despite the drought there is water for flowers,' he observed.

'Better to go hungry than starve for beauty,' Cameca replied and snipped off two roses which she handed to the Doctor.

'Thank you.' He sniffed them appreciatively. 'An aroma worthy of the gods.' He looked around the garden. 'Such a delightful place, this, though I imagine watering it must be quite a task.'

Cameca smiled. 'There is a tunnel under the garden,' she explained, 'and from it are small pipes which lead to the lawns and flower-beds.' She pointed to a nozzle with a watering rose on it which stuck up just above the ground. 'Water from the city's irrigation aqueducts fills a reservoir with a sluice-gate near the back wall. When the sluice-gate is opened the whole garden can be sprayed.'

'How ingenious,' the Doctor remarked as he sat down on a stone bench. 'I find it so restful here,' he said, 'so very restful.'

'It is the garden of peace.'

'Aptly named.'

'The words of Chapal.'

'Chapal?'

'He built the temple.'

'And set out the garden as well?' But the Doctor's mind was clicking over in another direction.

'As a labour of love,' Cameca replied.

'One senses that immediately. Does he ever come here?' The Doctor was all innocence.

'He watches over the garden constantly.'

‘Really?’ the Doctor’s face lit up.
‘In spirit.’
The Doctor’s face fell.
‘As does his son,’ Cameca continued.
‘Dead as well.’ The Doctor was despondent.
‘His son’s son lives.’
The Doctor cheered up a mite. ‘He’s a builder?’
‘No. A warrior.’
‘But perhaps he knows something of his grandfather’s work.’ The Doctor looked up at the pyramid. ‘I find the temple fascinating: the interior, the steps, the stairs, the antechambers.’ He stopped short of mentioning the tomb.
‘A meeting between you can be arranged,’ Cameca said.
Holding his roses, the Doctor stood up and bowed over her hand. ‘Dear lady, I would be eternally grateful,’ he said.

3

Chosen Warriors

Ian walked along the broad avenue with Tlotoxl limping at his side. The avenue was lined with windowless, one storey, box-like houses. Their entrances were elaborate wrought-iron gates, through which Ian could see the short passageway that led to the central, open-air courtyard with its lawn, flower-bed and tumbling bougainvillea. Around the courtyard were the rooms of the house. Ian thought that if ever he were to reach home again he would like to build a house like that. But then he remembered the considerable difference between the Mexican climate and the weather in England.

The Aztecs they passed on the way to the barracks bowed respectfully to Tlotoxl, but Ian sensed they were afraid of the High Priest.

'Do you often leave the temple?' he asked.

'Autloc seeks wisdom in the garden from time to time,' Tlotoxl replied. 'I visit the barracks to select a victim when the Gods demand blood.'

Ian felt his run cold.

The barracks was similar to the houses in design, but infinitely larger, and the central courtyard was an area of hard-baked clay where the warriors trained in the martial arts. When Ian and Tlotoxl entered the courtyard some two hundred warriors were at drill. They wore leather loin-cloths, sandals and plumed head-dresses. They carried shields and lunged with short swords, parrying attacks from imaginary enemies. When the Aztec in charge saw Tlotoxl, he ordered the warriors to stop and they stood respectfully as the High Priest of Sacrifice limped across the courtyard followed by Ian, who quickly became aware that the word had been passed by the warriors in the temple and everyone knew who he was. Suddenly Tlotoxl stopped, glanced along the ranks and pointed to a young warrior. Then he limped on to the far side of the courtyard. As they approached it, a warrior broke from the ranks and ran to open the door for them. There was a short passageway which opened onto another clay courtyard, patterned with the eagle and coiled snake in colourful dyes. Ian noticed that the courtyard was about the same size as the ones he had seen in the houses. There was a door in each of the other three walls. The two doors which faced one another were ornate, and decorated, once again, with the eagle and snake motif. The third door was made of plain wood.

Tlotoxl went to the centre of the courtyard. 'Ixta,' he called.

One of the decorated doors opened and a well-built, handsome man, a few years younger than Ian, came into the courtyard. He was wearing a leather loin-cloth with rectangular shapes embroidered on it in gold and silver thread. He wore sandals and his hair was drawn back in a short pony-tail. He bowed to Tlotoxl.

'I greet the High Priest of Sacrifice,' he said, then eyed Ian up and down. 'What manner of warrior is this?' His tone was disdainful.

'He is the servant of Yetaxa,' Tlotoxl replied.

Ixta bowed. 'I have heard that Yetaxa again guides us in wisdom and in strength. Does the High Priest wish me to demonstrate my skill to Yetaxa's servant?'

Tlotoxl inclined his head and Ixta strode to the door which opened onto the large courtyard.

'A warrior – one of the best,' he commanded.

The Aztec in charge signalled to a warrior, who ran to the door and entered the small courtyard.

'We shall fight with studded clubs and shields,' Ixta announced and led the warrior over to the plain wooden door. They went inside.

'To command one must prove courage, skill and intelligence.' Tlotoxl's voice was insinuating. Ixta had killed and taken many prisoners on the battlefield, he told Ian. 'He has no fear of death.'

Ixta and the warrior reappeared. Each carried a shield and a wooden cudgel which had a circular head studded with pieces of obsidian stone. They approached Tlotoxl, bowed to him, then went to the centre of the courtyard and stood facing one another, about ten feet apart. Just out of reach, Ian thought.

Tlotoxl raised one hand. 'Commence,' he commanded.

The two men circled each other warily. Then Ixta suddenly lunged and aimed a blow at the warrior's left-hand side. But as the warrior brought his shield across his body to fend off the cudgel, Ixta reversed his attack and hit out at the warrior's unprotected right. The warrior was swift and leapt back. Ixta swung at empty air, almost throwing himself off balance. Instinctively, he raised his shield to protect his head as the warrior's cudgel crashed down. As it struck the shield, Ixta gave a backhand chop just below the warrior's rib-cage. Blood spurted from the wound. The contestants backed away and circled each other again. Ian had anticipated a friendly encounter, but now he wasn't so sure. His mouth went dry and he gave a sideways glance at Tlotoxl beside him. The High Priest's face was expressionless. I shouldn't be surprised, Ian thought. He's accustomed to the sight of blood. Then Ixta launched a ferocious attack, forcing the warrior to give ground as he tried to ward off the repeated blows. The warrior tried to counterattack, but Ixta's shield was all around his body, protecting it until the last blow, which Ixta parried with his cudgel and with such force that the warrior's weapon flew from his hand and he was driven back trying to defend himself. Eventually he fell to his knees in a corner of the courtyard, with the shield held above his head. Ixta smashed his cudgel down on the warrior's shield and stepped back.

'Go and have your wound healed,' he said, and then walked over to Tlotoxl.

'Thus shall other tribes fear even more the Aztecs,' the High Priest said.

Ixta inclined his head and turned to Ian. 'Tell Yetaxa that I shall serve well.'

'I shall carry that salutation for you,' Tlotoxl replied. 'Yetaxa's servant remains here.'

Ixta looked puzzled. 'But here dwell only those chosen to command,' he said.

'I know it.' Tlotoxl looked from one to the other.

Ixta turned to Ian and there was fierce pride in his face. 'What name did your mother give you?' he asked.

'Ian.'

'Then I tell you, Ian, that six other warriors have dwelt in there,' he pointed to the other decorated door, 'but I alone remain. Yet I welcome you. There is no fear of you in me. And one day all men will fear Ixta, the Aztec commander who defeated the chosen servant of Yetaxa.'

Ian did not reply, but met Ixta's arrogant gaze with a look he hoped was steadfast.

'Let him be clothed according to his rank,' Tlotoxl said.

'It shall be done,' Ixta replied and asked if Ian would assist at the Rain God's ceremony.

'He is now as you are, Ixta, a chosen warrior,' the High Priest replied and limped out of the courtyard.

'What am I supposed to do at this ceremony?' Ian asked.

'All honour rests with us,' Ixta's voice rang with pride, 'we deliver the human sacrifice to the High Priest Tlotoxl,' and then in a matter-of-fact voice added that it was time to obtain Ian's uniform.

Ian stood dumbfounded.

Cameca had gone home, leaving a contemplative Doctor in the garden. She returned later with a tray, on which were cornflower pancakes, a jar of honey, a knife, two goblets and a jug of water. Cameca put the tray on the bench where the Doctor was sitting, and then sat down herself. The Doctor had eaten two pancakes with honey and drunk a goblet of water when he saw a cloaked, plumed Aztec warrior with an embroidered loin-cloth and sandals striding purposefully towards him. It took the Doctor a full fifteen seconds to recognise Ian.

'Ah, Chesterton,' he called, his eyes sparkling with amusement at Ian's clothes, 'have a pancake and honey.' Ian declined and the Doctor introduced him to Cameca whom, he added, had promised to arrange a meeting between himself and the grandson of the man who built the temple.

'That is most kind of you, madam,' Ian smiled at Cameca, who returned his smile though her eyes looked momentarily troubled. She glanced down at the tray and then at the Doctor.

He gently patted his stomach. 'Delicious and plenteous, dear lady.'

Cameca stood and picked up the tray. The Doctor also rose to his feet.

'Pray excuse me,' Cameca said, 'then you may talk more freely.' She walked away.

'Nice person, Chesterton, gentle and . . .'

'Doctor,' Ian's voice rang with urgency, 'today there's to be a human sacrifice at the Rain God ceremony and I'm supposed to assist. I can't possibly do it.'

The Doctor put his hand on Ian's shoulder. 'Just a minute, Chesterton,' he said, 'what exactly must you do?'

'Escort the victim to the altar.'

'Then do it.' The Doctor spoke brusquely.

Ian was appalled. 'You can't expect me to participate in murder.'

'Intervene and we'll be dead within the minute.'

'But,' Ian began in desperation.

'No buts about it,' the Doctor cut in, 'if human sacrifice is their tradition, then let them get on with it.' He removed his arm from Ian's shoulder and pointed a forefinger at Ian's chest. 'For your own sake, for Barbara's, for Susan's and for mine, do not interfere.' These last words were spoken in a measured tone. 'Promise me, Ian,' the Doctor insisted.

Ian looked down at the ground. 'All right, you have my word,' he murmured.

The Doctor patted him on the arm. 'I'll go and tell Barbara,' he said, and hurried away. It was only when he entered the pyramid that he remembered all the stairs he had to climb.

Susan and Barbara were in the antechamber below the temple. Barbara had taken off her sandals and lay on a couch wriggling her toes while munching a banana. 'Hardly god-like behaviour,' she remarked between bites to Susan who was trying on Barbara's plumed crown.

'What do you think?' Susan asked as she struck a fashion-photo pose.

'It's just the thing for the Royal Enclosure at Ascot,' Barbara replied and they both laughed.

'I enjoy being the handmaiden of a god,' Susan said.

'This end isn't too hard to take, either,' Barbara admitted.

Susan took off the head-dress and put it down on a legless side-table beside a highly polished jade statuette of an Aztec god. Susan picked it up. 'Look at this,' she said, 'it's exquisite.'

'That's the type of thing which hooked me on the Aztec civilisation in the first place,' Barbara replied, placing the banana skin on the plate at her side. 'On the one hand, there's Autloc who is charming, intelligent and cultured. But, on the other hand . . .'

'There's Tlotoxl,' Susan interjected. 'Strange, isn't it? Such beauty and such horror existing side by side.'

As she replaced the statuette, they heard the Doctor's breathless voice outside the antechamber.

'Let me pass,' he was saying, gasping for air, 'go on, out of my way, I must talk to Yetaxa.'

Barbara stood up as Susan went to the door and opened it.

The Doctor stumbled in. 'Wait outside, Susan,' he gasped, 'and don't let anyone in.'

'Yes, grandfather.' Susan left, closing the door behind her.

'Sit down, Doctor, and catch your breath.' Barbara motioned to a couch.

The Doctor collapsed onto it. 'All those stairs, all those stairs.' He took a deep breath and Barbara poured him a goblet of water which he gulped down.

Barbara waited until he had recovered. 'What is it, Doctor? What's happened?'

The Doctor stood up. 'There's to be a human sacrifice during the Rain God ceremony at sunset.' He kept all emotion out of his voice.

'Oh, no!' Barbara was horrified. 'No!'

'You must not interfere, do you understand me?'

Barbara buried her face in her hands. 'I can't stand by and . . .'

'You must.' The Doctor barked out the two words, then his voice softened. 'Ian agrees with me,' he paused before continuing, 'and he is required to escort the victim to the altar.'

Barbara's hands flew from her face. 'He has to do what?' she exploded.

'He's been designated a Chosen Warrior' – the

Doctor shrugged – 'and for all our sakes, he has agreed, given me his word, to do nothing to prevent the sacrifice.'

'Well, I have been made a god,' Barbara paced out her words, 'and I forbid it.'

'Barbara,' the Doctor began to protest, but Barbara cut him off.

'No, Doctor. There will be no sacrifice at sunset, nor ever again. The reincarnation of Yetaxa will prove to the Aztec people that you don't need to cut out a pulsating human heart to make the rain come.'

'Don't be foolish, woman. The High Priests will turn on you and denounce you.'

'They won't dare to defy me,' Barbara replied with great determination. 'No, this is the beginning of the end of Huitzilipochtli's reign.'

'What on earth are you talking about?' the Doctor demanded.

'Rewriting history,' Barbara said calmly. 'If I can start the destruction of all that is evil here, then all that is good will survive when Cortez lands.'

The Doctor shook his head in bewilderment and spread out his arms. 'You can't change history, Barbara. Not one line of it.'

Barbara turned her back on him, went to the side-table, picked up her plumed crown and set it on her head.

'I appeal to you, Barbara. Be reasonable. What you're trying is impossible,' the Doctor implored, 'believe me, I know, really I do, I know.'

She turned to face him and was quite serene. 'Not Barbara,' she said calmly, 'Yetaxa.'

4

Sacrifice to Tlaloc

In full regalia Ian and Ixta left the barracks with the warrior Tlotoxl had chosen as his sacrifice. He wore only a loin-cloth, sandals and a plumed head-dress. He had been fed an adequate amount of a drug which dulled his senses to reality and enlivened his desire to join the gods. Storm clouds gathered in the sky. Rain would fall with or without the brutal death of this young man and Ian wondered if he could slow down their pace so that, with any luck, it might start before they reached the altar. But Ixta and the warrior maintained an Aztec's pace and Ian had no choice but to keep step with them. To his surprise the streets were deserted, the city silent. He discovered the reason when they turned into the broad avenue that led to the pyramid. The square in front of it was packed. Ian estimated that there must have been between ten and fifteen thousand people – men, women and children. As the three of them approached, the crowd parted, opening up a path for them to the entrance of the pyramid. All eyes were on them and there was absolute silence apart from the sound of their sandals as they marched to the open door and went inside, the warrior first, then Ixta, and after him, Ian, who realised that the palms of his hands were soaked with sweat.

Susan was standing with a temple guard outside the antechamber when she heard footsteps. She looked up the stairs that led to the temple. Both High Priests were descending. Susan opened the antechamber door and went inside. The Doctor and Barbara were facing each other in stony silence.

'The High Priests are coming,' she whispered.

The Doctor pointed his forefinger at Barbara. 'Be warned, young woman,' he growled.

Susan was about to ask what was happening when the High Priests entered the antechamber. They bowed.

'The temple awaits your presence, Great Spirit of Yetaxa,' Autloc addressed her.

'My handmaiden remains here.' Barbara pointed to Susan.

'As Yetaxa decrees,' Tlotoxl replied.

'However, Yetaxa's aged servant will accompany the Great Spirit to the temple,' the Doctor said, and Barbara did not fail to note the hint of menace in his voice.

'We shall be honoured by his presence,' said Autloc.

Steeling herself for what she intended to do, Barbara walked regally from the room, followed by the two High Priests and then the Doctor, who turned to Susan just before he left.

'Stay here, child,' he warned.

A guard drew back the brocade curtain and let Barbara and the others into the temple. The walls and the terrace were lined with Aztec warriors. As Barbara approached the throne she looked furtively about her for Ian. There was no sign of him. She sat down and gazed before her. Tlotoxl's obsidian knife lay glinting on the sacrificial altar. The two High Priests moved onto the terrace and Autloc raised his arms.

'A vision has come to us, my people,' he intoned, 'the High Priest Yetaxa has returned so that you may look again on the sign of the coiled serpent.' The Doctor thought that the whole ceremony would be ridiculous if it were not so gruesome, as no one two hundred and fifty feet below in the square could possibly hear a word Autloc said.

But Susan in the antechamber below heard and, defying her grandfather's command, she went up the stairs and peeped through the curtain.

Autloc turned to Barbara. 'Great Spirit of Yetaxa, step forth that we may honour you.'

Barbara stood and walked slowly out onto the terrace with Autloc at her side. She stood on the edge of the parapet, spread out her arms and looked down at the sea of faces staring up at her. There was not a sound, and the sky was dark and heavy with clouds. She returned to the throne and sat down. The Doctor with a slight inclination of his head signalled his approval.

'Bring forth the sacrifice to Tlaloc,' Tlotoxl commanded. Barbara's hands gripped the arms of the throne. Two Aztecs pulled back the second brocade curtain behind which Ian, Ixta and the warrior stood. As the warrior came into the temple, he bowed to Barbara. Ian and Ixta, following him, did the same, but Ian and Barbara's eyes met in an expression of sheer horror.

Tlotoxl picked up the obsidian knife and the warrior lay down on the altar.

'Take his arms,' Tlotoxl ordered Ixta, and then to Ian, 'take his legs.'

Before he obeyed, Ian glanced at the Doctor, who looked away in distress.

Tlotoxl raised the knife above his head to the cloud-laden sky. 'Great Tlaloc, God of Water, I, Tlotoxl, High

Priest of Sacrifice, call upon you to look down upon our land with favour. Give us the water that is our life,' his voice rose to a screeching crescendo, 'and we shall honour you with blood!'

Susan screamed and ran into the temple as Barbara leapt to her feet.

'Stop, Tlotoxl, I, Yetaxa command you!'

The High Priest's hands were quivering with frustration as he spun around to face Barbara.

'Let no more blood be spilt.' She looked at Ian and Ixta. 'Release him.'

The warrior jumped to his feet as they obeyed and he went angrily to the throne. 'You have denied me honour,' he accused her.

'Then honour Tlaloc with your death,' Tlotoxl said.

The young warrior looked at the High Priest, then ran to the edge of the parapet, threw himself off and hurtled to his death two hundred and fifty feet below.

Barbara sat down in shock, then there was a blinding flash of lightning, a clap of thunder and the rain came down in torrents.

Tlotoxl leered victoriously at Barbara. 'With death came rain,' he proclaimed.

'Without your sacrifice came rain,' Barbara replied as steadily as she could.

Tlotoxl glanced slyly at Susan as he limped over to the throne. 'Does Yetaxa speak as a God or the protector of a handmaiden?'

'As a God.'

Tlotoxl's hand, still holding the obsidian knife, shot out and pointed to Susan. 'Then your handmaiden must be punished. She cried out and desecrated the temple. She transgressed the law.'

'She did not know it.'

'Then let knowledge be beaten into her.'

Barbara stood up and went to Susan's side. 'No one shall be punished for an offence committed in ignoance.'

'I demand that she be punished,' Tlotoxl snarled.

'No,' Barbara was adamant, but she knew a compromise had to be reached. 'Let her instead be taught respect for your customs.'

Autloc stepped forward. 'I shall take her to the seminary,' he said.

Barbara smiled at him. 'So be it, Autloc.'

'The Great Spirit of Yetaxa has spoken.' He bowed and led Susan from the temple.

Tlotoxl turned away and went out onto the terrace, where he stood in the pouring rain. He held the obsidian knife in both hands and placed the tip on the altar. 'No, no, this is not Yetaxa who speaks,' he murmured, the rain streaming down his face. 'This is a false god whom I must destroy.' He stabbed at the altar with the knife and the blade broke.

As soon as she was back in the antechamber, Barbara took off her head-dress, threw it to one side, slumped onto a couch and toyed with the coiled snake on her wrist.

The Doctor stood over her.

'Well, young woman, are you satisfied, happy with your day's work?'

Barbara stared at the carpeted floor, fighting back the tears which welled up in her eyes.

'You wouldn't be advised, would you?' the Doctor persisted, 'dear me, no, you knew better.'

'I couldn't sit there and watch that young man being sacrificed,' Barbara's voice was choked and she bit on her lower lip.

'Do you think we felt differently?' the Doctor snapped.

Barbara shook her head in misery.

'Then why didn't you leave well alone? Human sacrifice is part of their religion and there is nothing we can do about it.'

'I had to try.' She was barely audible.

'And look at the result. Tlotoxl has certainly lost faith in you, which puts all our lives in danger and Susan is locked up in some sort of school.'

'At least she's safe there.' Barbara swallowed hard.

'She was perfectly safe here until you started meddling.'

Barbara clenched her fists. 'I wanted it to rain without that young man being killed.'

'Barbara, he wanted to be offered to the Gods. It made him one as well.'

The tears began to trickle down her cheeks. 'I didn't think about it in those terms.'

'You just didn't think,' the Doctor retorted angrily.

Barbara buried her face in her hands, her body wracked with sobs. The Doctor stood by uncomfortably and his anger turned in on himself. He had been unreasonable and he knew it. Barbara's experience of travelling through time and space was extremely limited, his was considerable to say the least. He could become a Babylonian deity at the drop of his hat, but for Barbara to have the role of an Aztec god thrust upon her must be very difficult indeed. He went to the couch and sat down beside her.

'Oh, please, please, just go away,' she sobbed, 'and leave me alone.'

Instead the Doctor put his arm around her shoulder and with his other hand took a large handkerchief from his pocket. 'I'm sorry, my dear,' he said gently, 'I shouldn't have been so harsh with you.'

Barbara looked at him through her tears and shook

her head. 'No, I'm crying because you were quite right.'

'Here, dry your eyes.' The Doctor offered her his handkerchief. She took it, dabbed her eyes, wiped her cheeks, and sniffed.

'What have I done to us?' she asked, tugging at the handkerchief.

'It's done now,' the Doctor shrugged, 'but what happens next is also up to you.'

'Me?' Barbara looked surprised.

The Doctor tapped the palm of one hand with his other fist. 'Hold off Tlotoxl,' he said.

'How can I? As you've just said, he has no faith in me.'

'But Autloc does.' The Dotor had a glint in his eyes which Barbara had seen before.

'You want me to play them off against each other,' she ventured.

The Doctor nodded. 'Yes, Barbara. The more Tlotoxl doubts you, the more you must convince Autloc that you are Yetaxa.'

'You believe Sacrifice won't dare defy Knowledge.'

'You saw for yourself, my dear. Tlotoxl wanted Susan beaten, but when Autloc suggested taking her to the seminary he gave way.'

'What about you and Ian?'

The Doctor waved a hand in the air. 'Ian can take care of himself,' he assured her. He then told her that, in the garden, he had chanced upon an Aztec lady who knew indirectly how the temple was constructed. He straighteneded his tie and winked at her. 'I'll soon find out about the entrance to the tomb.'

'Doctor, you're an old rogue,' Barbara rebuked him with a smile.

'But really, Barbara, it's up to you. As long as you are here, and they trust you, we are reasonably safe.'

'I understand,' she replied.

The antechamber door opened and Tlotoxl limped into the room. Barbara and the Doctor remained seated.

'You enter unannounced,' Barbara said haughtily.

'I proclaim myself only to my Gods,' Tlotoxl replied and looked at the Doctor. 'Let the old man go down to the garden.'

The Doctor noted that he had been relegated from the aged servant of Yetaxa to an old man.

'Enjoy the company of your new-found friend,' Barbara said as the Doctor stood up, bowed and muttered his obedience to Yetaxa's commands.

Tlotoxl waited until the Doctor had left the room, then looked at Barbara with naked hatred in his eyes. 'I would ask you' – he spat out the words – 'how shall a man know his Gods?'

Barbara held out her wrist with the bracelet on it. 'By the signs of their divinity,' she replied.

'And if thieves walk among the Gods?'

'Then, indeed, how shall a man know,' she conceded.

'By the secrets of the Gods' minds,' Tlotoxl stabbed a finger repeatedly against the side of his head.

'It is true,' Barbara agreed that their knowledge would reveal them.

'How many heavens are there?' Tlotoxl snapped.

Barbara laughed. 'Does the High Priest of Sacrifice covet the mantle of the High Priest of Knowledge?' Her voice was light.

'How many heavens?' he snarled.

'Thirteen.' Barbara was grateful for her interest in Aztec culture.

'Name them.'

'If the truth of my divinity lies hidden in my mind, let Autloc seek it,' she replied.

'So he shall.' Tlotoxl's voice was full of malevolence. 'Just as the chosen warrior, whose grandfather built this temple, shall challenge your servant.'

'To what purpose?' Barbara asked.

Tlotoxl stared into her eyes. 'To determine which one of them will survive to command the Aztec armies.'

Barbara was shaken. She knew the shock had shown in her eyes, and she also knew that Tlotoxl had seen it.

5

Perfect Victim

The life-size clay model of a warrior wore a loin-cloth, sandals and a head-dress. On its chest was a small red circle to indicate the heart. Ixta stood at the other end of the courtyard holding a javelin, which he threw with devastating accuracy into the circle. Ian, who was watching with Autloc, thought Ixta would be a useful addition to a darts team. Ixta swaggered over to them, his right hand on the hilt of the short sword hanging at his side.

'Thus shall my enemies fall,' he said arrogantly.

'Real enemies can hit back,' Ian remarked quietly.

'I have no fear of death,' Ixta retorted.

'Perhaps not. The dead never win.'

Autloc looked sharply at Ian. 'How would you attack?' he asked.

'A little more cunningly,' Ian replied, 'I'd use stealth to surprise my enemy.'

'This also I can do.' Ixta spun around and when they were face to face again, the sword was drawn and the tip touching Ian's stomach.

Ian smiled at Ixta as the chosen warrior slid the sword

back into its scabbard. Ian held up his left thumb. 'This is all I need,' he said casually.

Autloc looked surprised and observed that to win a victory with a thumb would require magic.

Ian shook his head. 'Knowing your enemy's weakness isn't magic,' he said, 'it's commonsense.'

Ixta laughed and pointed to himself. 'What weakness have I that is vunerable to your thumb?'

'You'd be surprised,' Ian replied.

Ixta hesitated, doubt in his eyes.

'Don't worry, Ixta, I won't kill you. Not this time.' Ian remained composed; Autloc was intrigued and Ixta bristled.

'You mock the arts of war and I defy you to harm me,' he challenged.

Ian looked at the studded club that lay on the ground beside them. 'Pick up the club, Ixta,' Ian pointed to it with his left thumb.

Ixta eyed Ian suspiciously and then bent down to pick up the cudgel with his right hand. But he never quite reached it, as Ian was astride him from behind and had clamped Ixta's right arm in a half-nelson hold, leaving him powerless to pick up the cudgel or draw his sword. At the same time Ian rammed his left thumb onto the pressure point behind Ixta's left ear. For a few seconds Ixta thrashed vainly with his left arm to disengage Ian's thumb, and then went limp. Ian released him and Ixta slumped to the ground. Autloc stared at Ian in astonishment.

'Give him a little time,' Ian smiled at the High Priest, 'he'll soon wake up.'

At that moment Tlotoxl limped into the courtyard. 'Autloc, there is a task to be . . .' he stopped short when he saw Ixta.

Autloc turned to him. 'He sleeps. Yetaxa's servant

won the victory with his thumb.'

Tlotoxl looked warily at Ian and turned back to Autloc. 'You saw the blow?'

'There was no blow.' Autloc held up his left thumb. 'He defeated Ixta with this.'

'Tell him to rest until the sun has passed the zenith,' Ian advised as he walked away.

'Where do you go?' Autloc asked.

'For a stroll,' Ian was enjoying himself.

'I shall accompany you,' and the two of them left the courtyard.

Ixta stirred, propped himself up on his elbows, shook his head and exercised his neck muscles.

Tlotoxl looked down at him. 'Could you not fight against it?'

'I was powerless.' Ixta rose groggily to his feet and leaned against the courtyard wall. 'My strength was drained from me like that,' and he snapped his fingers.

Tlotoxl was disconcerted.

Tonila, a small, portly, balding Priest of Knowledge waddled, posy in hand, into the courtyard, bowed to Tlotoxl and announced that the Perfect Victim desired to be admitted.

'All his requests must be granted,' Tlotoxl replied, and as Tonila left he reiterated quietly, 'must be granted.'

The Perfect Victim entered the courtyard. He was a handsome youth of eighteen and his white loin-cloth and cloak were hemmed with gold thread, which had also been used to weave the eagle and coiled-snake motif on the back of his cloak. Even his sandals were white.

'You grace the Chosen Warriors' barracks by your presence.' Tlotoxl gestured towards Ixta. 'Here is one who would be commander of our armies.'

'Ixta, I have heard of your valour and your skill,' the

Perfect Victim exclaimed, and then looked puzzled. 'Why do you say "would be" when all know he is to be the commander?'

'There are some who say the accounts of his deeds and the truth are far apart,' Tlotoxl replied, looking slyly at Ixta, who was furious.

'No man can win against me,' he shouted.

'None, not one?' Tlotoxl sneered.

'I shall lead our armies,' Ixta replied stubbornly. 'It is my right.'

'Yesterday it seemed so,' Tlotoxl remarked dryly.

Ixta glared at him, picked up the cudgel, stomped off to the centre of the courtyard and began practising swings and blows.

Tonila looked with surprise at the High Priest of Sacrifice.

'You would make an enemy?' he asked naively.

'I?' Tlotoxl protested. 'I only know that I have seen a man who could defeat him.'

'Defeat Ixta?' The Perfect Victim could hardly believe his ears.

Ixta stopped swinging the cudgel and turned towards them. 'Once. And that by a trick.' He pointed the cudgel at Tlotoxl. 'I tell you that face to face, I can pull the stranger down.'

'Perhaps.'

'You drive the man.' The Perfect Victim's voice was reproachful. 'How often have you and Autloc instructed me that small failings in a man may be his saving graces?'

'But you, oh Perfect Victim, are as your name implies,' Tlotoxl replied. 'When the time is ripe and you face the Gods, all failings will have dropped away. How else could you meet the Gods to tell them of the Aztecs?' He paused dramatically and then raised his voice. 'Should not the commander of our armies be equally pure so that his very name will strike awe and dread in our enemies' camps?'

The Perfect Victim considered the High Priest's argument and nodded. 'He who defeated Ixta should command.'

'No!' Ixta roared.

Tlotoxl raised a calming hand and conceded that Yetaxa's servant may have won through trickery. 'A second contest would resolve the matter but I cannot order it,' he shrugged his shoulders and waited for Tonila, in his simplicity, to come to the rescue.

'The Perfect Victim's desires must be fulfilled at all times,' he burbled.

Tlotoxl clenched his fists in delight as the Perfect Victim went to Ixta's side.

'My faith in Ixta is supreme,' the young man said, 'and it is my desire the Chosen Warriors meet in contest once again.'

'As the sun sets, I shall arrange it,' Tlotoxl promised, and then casually expressed his opinion that two men fought better when one challenged the other as there was less vigour in a contest made for entertainment.

'I shall challenge the stranger,' said Ixta.

'Let it be so,' the Perfect Victim said, and left the courtyard with Tonila.

Tlotoxl limped to Ixta's side and whispered in his ear. 'This I promise you, all honour and glory shall be yours if you destroy him.'

The Doctor and Cameca were in the garden looking at the flowers and plants. The Doctor touched a leaf and asked her what it was.

'It is herbal and the sap of the stem is used by those who practise medicine to induce sleep.'

'I think I know of it,' the Doctor replied, straightening

up. As he did so, he scratched the back of his hand on a thorn of the maguey cactus plant which grew beside the herb. 'Ouch!' He put the back of his hand to his mouth. Cameca laughed and suggested that Yetaxa's aged servant might care to sleep until the wound healed. The Doctor declined, smiling, and they walked on along the path.

'What do you call yourself?' Cameca asked.

'I'm known as the Doctor, but I am not a healer. I am a scientist, an engineer, a builder of things.'

'Now I understand your interest in the pyramid and the temple.'

The Doctor admitted that there were several details concerning the interior that intrigued him and this time came straight to the point.

'Yetaxa's tomb, for example, is sealed, but surely the builder, now what was his name . . . ah . . . Chalap . . .'

'Chapal,' Cameca said.

'Yes, of course,' the Doctor replied. 'Surely he devised a way of opening it.'

Cameca admitted that her knowledge of the pyramid was insufficient to answer his query, but she was sure Chapal's grandson would know the answer.

The Doctor stopped and sniffed an exotic flower. 'Such fragrance,' he murmured and added that he didn't want to pry into what might be a family secret.

'No one could think that of you,' she replied. 'When shall the meeting be?'

'Oh, any time.' The Doctor was nonchalant. 'Today?'

Cameca observed that an interested mind brooked no delay.

The Doctor looked at her and smiled. 'I'm sure that's true of you, Cameca.'

She blushed. 'It was once. Now I'm content to pass the time of day here like the others.'

'Their minds are old, dear lady, something yours will never be,' the Doctor protested.

Cameca smiled. 'Your heart too is young, Doctor.' She touched his hand and said she would go and see the builder's grandson at once.

As she hurried away the Doctor sighed. He had a sense of guilt because, much as he liked Cameca, he knew he was using her. And does the end justify the means, he asked himself. In this instance, definitely, yes; the thought was resolute, but the guilt still niggled.

Barbara received the High Priest of Sacrifice in the temple. Seated on the throne, she was determined to draw on all the divinity she could muster. She looked down at Tlotoxl and waited for him to speak.

'The High Priest of Knowledge will question you.'

'And if he finds I am the Spirit of Yetaxa returned, what then?'

'I shall beg forgiveness of the Gods for my unworthy doubts.'

'I will remember the words of the High Priest of Sacrifice.'

Tlotoxl leant towards the throne, his impenetrable eyes glistening. 'Remember this also.' His voice was a menace. 'Whilst your divinity is in dispute, only those who serve the temple may approach you.'

'My servant also,' Barbara protested.

'No!' Tlotoxl spat out the word. 'You are to remain alone.'

'For what reason?' Barbara enquired calmly.

'A false God's servants would conspire against us,' Tlotoxl said accusingly. 'Such a danger we are not prepared to tolerate.'

'Then let my servants be told they may not enter here,' Barbara replied evenly.

'It will be done,' Tlotoxl replied and limped out of the temple leaving a very disquieted Barbara behind him.

Cameca was walking along the broad avenue on her way to the barracks when a messenger approached her. He bowed respectfully and said that Ixta, the Chosen Warrior, sought her counsel. Cameca smiled and replied that she would go directly to his quarters.

She came into the courtyard and went over to Ixta's door, which was open. She called his name and Ixta invited her in.

The quarters consisted of three small rooms. On one side of the central living area was the bathroom, essential to most dwellings, as the Aztecs, with the exception of High Priests of Sacrifice, bathed two or three times a day. On the other side was the bedroom with a woven straw mattress on the floor and two wicker-work trunks for Ixta's loin-cloths and cloaks. His head-dresses were kept on a shelf, his sandals underneath it. The main room had a legless square wooden table with a cushion at each side. Ixta pointed to a cushion and Cameca sat down. Ixta sat facing her.

'I was told you wish to see me, Ixta.'

'I would seek your advice, Cameca.'

'If I can give it, I shall,' she replied.

Ixta rubbed behind his left ear with his thumb and asked what she knew of magic.

'Nothing,' Cameca admitted, 'though it is my belief I know one who does.'

Ixta leaned forward. 'What name has this person?'

'He is known as the Doctor and is the aged servant of Yetaxa.'

Ixta dismissed the suggestion with a wave of his hand. 'He is of no use to me.'

'You may be of service to him,' Cameca said. 'He

seeks an interview with you.'

Ixta was curious. 'To what end?'

'He is interested in your lamented father's father's work. In particular the temple,' she added.

Ixta ran his hand across his face. 'Does he know my name?' he asked abruptly.

'No.'

'Do not reveal it, but say that I shall meet him.' His voice was casual.

'Where?'

'Does he not spend his day in the temple garden?'

Cameca nodded.

'Then there, I shall pass by after the sun is over the zenith and my food has been brought to me.' He stood up and helped Cameca to her feet.

'I shall deliver those words, Ixta.' She felt pleased to have been of service to the Doctor, as she liked his company.

'Be mindful not to reveal my name,' Ixta called to her from the doorway as Cameca crossed the courtyard. Then he went back into the room chuckling. There was no better way to destroy one's enemies than to let them destroy themselves.

6

Thorn of Doom

The cell Susan occupied at the seminary was one of several which opened onto a cloister. It was a small room with only a woven straw mattress, a wicker-work trunk and a cushion for furniture. She wore a full-length simple grey robe with short sleeves, and a multi-coloured sash tied around her waist. She sat on the cushion looking up at Autloc, who stood in front of her.

'You have been taught the code of the good housewife and committed it to memory?' the High Priest asked.

'I have,' Susan replied.

'Let me hear it.'

'Tend well your nurseries and your flowerbeds. Keep clean your pot and stewpan,' she recited, 'do not spend recklessly, do not destroy or cheapen yourself.' She hesitated, thinking about the word 'destroy' and Tlotoxl.

'You will never have –' Autloc prompted as Tonila came into the cell.

'Oh, yes. You will never have a house or a home of your own if you live like that,' she rattled off. Tonila nodded approvingly and remarked that Susan had learnt it diligently. Susan wondered if the Priest of Knowledge would like to know about Einstein's theory of relativity.

Autloc praised her as a good pupil who used her intelligence and then introduced Tonila. Susan stood up and went to shake hands.

'You do not greet your elders in such a manner,' Autloc reproached her, 'you stand still, not looking around. Your eyes see only the person to whom you are being introduced,' he made a small gesture with his posy, 'unless you are meeting for the first time your prospective husband, in which case you keep your eyes downcast.'

'But how will I know?' Susan was intrigued.

'Know what, child?'

'That he's to be my husband.'

'You will be told,' Autloc stated very matter-of-factly.

'Told!' Susan exploded. 'No one's going to tell me who

to marry.'

Tonila was taken aback. 'What say have you in the matter?'

'It's my life,' Susan's voice was full of indignation, 'and I'll spend it with whom I choose, not someone picked out for me.'

Autloc was perturbed by her outburst. Young Aztec women accepted arranged marriages without question but if, as Yetaxa's handmaiden, Susan refused, that meant their traditional behaviour was contrary to the Gods' wishes. If this were so, then in how many other ways might they also be so acting? The seed of doubt was sown.

The Doctor was weeding a flowerbed when Ixta came into the garden. He strode over to the Doctor and identified himself as the grandson of Chapal, the man who built the temple. The Doctor straightened and looked at Ixta, who wore an ordinary warrior's loin-cloth and cloak, as well as a plumed battle-mask which concealed the upper half of his face.

'Ah!' the Doctor said, and expressed his admiration of the pyramid. 'The entrance to the tomb of the High Priest Yetaxa is a particularly fine piece of work.'

'Only the temples my father's father built have similar vaults,' Ixta replied.

'A secret design. All the best architects have one,' the Doctor remarked.

'A drawing exists,' Ixta said, adding that as his father and his grandfather were with the Gods it was in his possession.

'Would it be possible for me to see it?' the Doctor enquired.

'Can a humble warrior deny the request of Yetaxa's aged servant? I shall show it to you after sunset if the

Gods are willing.'

'Why shouldn't they be?'

The Doctor was curious and Ixta explained that he had to meet another warrior in combat just before the sun set.

'Not to the death, I trust?' the Doctor asked anxiously.

'No, but defeat would mean disgrace,' Ixta replied, 'and I would be confined to my quarters and no one might look upon me or speak to me for many days.'

The Doctor gave the problem his consideration.

'My opponent has been selected,' Ixta continued. 'I know his name and I fear defeat.'

The Doctor asked what weapons would be used.

Ixta spread out his hands. 'These alone, and my skills lie with a spear, sword or club.'

'Oh dear,' the Doctor sighed, 'and I really wanted to see the drawing.'

'No more than I desire a victory.'

The Doctor studied the scratch on the back of his hand. 'Then let us assist one another,' he said, and led Ixta to the maguey cactus plant. The Doctor broke off a thorn and then a shoot from the herb beside it. He began squeezing the sap from the stem onto the tip of the thorn.

'With this I shall win?' Ixta asked.

'Be careful not to scratch yourself with it,' the Doctor advised.

'The aged servant of Yetaxa proffers poison?'

'Not to kill.' The Doctor squeezed the last drop of sap onto the thorn. 'But used properly it will drain away your opponent's strength and he will sleep. Scratch here.' The Doctor drew it across the inside of his wrist and then handed the thorn to the Chosen Warrior.

'I thank you.' Ixta smiled.

'You won't forget the drawing, will you?'

'I shall be here after sunset.'

'So shall I.'

Ixta strode away and the Doctor sat on a bench thinking that a little knowledge of horticulture could, on occasion, take one a very long way.

Under Tlotoxl's appraising eyes, Ian stood in the middle of the courtyard swinging a cudgel in circles around his head and alongside his body, shifting it from hand to hand. It reminded him of working out with Indian clubs in a gymnasium – only this time he was not simply toning up his muscles but preparing himself for a battle that would mean life or death. Under Aztec law, he had defeated Ixta, but he knew that neither Tlotoxl nor the Chosen Warrior would accept it. He realised he was no match for Ixta with a spear – fighting with them he would be on the defensive, using his shield for protection. With cudgels he thought he stood a chance, but with his bare hands he knew he could win. He needed a strategy, a battle plan which would never give Ixta the advantage. The problem was to bring the contest to a wrestling match as quickly as possible so that he could use a mixture of techniques – all-in, judo and karate – of which he was confident the Aztecs knew nothing. He paused to consider the problem.

'Does fatigue affect the young man in Yetaxa's service?' Tlotoxl's voice was sardonic.

Ian looked at him evenly. 'Does the High Priest of Sacrifice scorn my attempts to prove my worthiness to command?' Ian picked up a second cudgel and began swinging both of them in a gymnasium routine. As the studded cudgels were heavier than Indian clubs his wrists soon began to ache but he was determined not to let Tlotoxl see any sign of it. Ixta came onto the courtyard and went to Tlotoxl's side as Ian stepped up his tempo.

'Can you conquer him, Ixta?' Tlotoxl murmured.

'I know it,' Ixta grinned and called to Ian, who stopped, secretly grateful, and turned to face him.

'Yes, Ixta?'

'I challenge you to a contest of strength.'

'A fight?'

'Without weapons. Your hands defeated me. Now let mine strive for victory over you.'

Ian was suspicious. He could not understand why Ixta would throw down the gauntlet where he had the least likelihood of success.

'Will you refuse him?' Tlotoxl's voice rasped.

'No,' Ian replied.

'Then we fight here as the sun sets.'

'All right.' Ian began to swing the cudgels again but his brain sought the reason behind the challenge.

'You are confident of victory?' Tlotoxl's eyes were fixed on Ian as he muttered the question to Ixta.

'If you wish it, he shall die,' Ixta replied.

Tlotoxl nodded. 'Let him die,' he said with a brushing-aside movement of his hand.

Barbara and Autloc were in the temple. She was standing beside the throne and the High Priest of Knowledge had been questioning her about Aztec mythology. Once again Barbara owed much to her studies at university.

'I shall tell the High Priest of Sacrifice that I am satisfied of your divinity,' Autloc said when the questioning was finished.

'That won't stop Tlotoxl.' Barbara smiled wryly. 'He is determined to destroy me.'

'He cannot whilst I believe you to be Yetaxa,' Autloc said gravely.

'Yet you question me at his bidding.'

'We both serve Huitzilipochtli.'

'Do you?' Barbara looked at him quizzically. 'Were you not angry when I forbade the sacrifice to the Rain God?'

'No.'

'Do you then question the necessity of human sacrifice?'

'I accept it. We send messengers to many Gods,' Autloc smiled at her, 'why should the Gods not send a messenger to us?'

'To say there must be no more human sacrifice,' Barbara suggested quietly. She walked around the throne running her right forefinger along the arm, over the back and along the other arm.

'I shall not oppose the Gods if it is their will that such sacrifices cease.'

'And Tlotoxl, what of him?'

'I have said we both serve Huitzilipochtli and through him other Gods whose biddings we obey.'

Barbara smiled at his serious face. 'The High Priest of Knowledge speaks with great wisdom.'

He studied his posy of flowers for a few seconds before replying. 'If your words are denied, shall we not be living in defiance of the Gods?' he asked.

Barbara went back mentally to her history books again and the end of the Aztec civilisation under the Spanish yoke. 'Famine, drought and disaster will come and more and more sacrifices will be made in supplication,' she said slowly, measuring out her words. 'I see a time to come when ten thousand warriors will die in one day under the obsidian knives of High Priests of Sacrifice.'

'In one day?' Autloc was deeply distressed.

Barbara thought about the Aztecs' last desperate bid

to turn the tide of battle in their favour, never fully realising that a loin-cloth, sandals, plumed head-dress, stabbing sword, studded cudgel, arrows and a shield were no match for armoured breastplates, boots, steel helmets, cannons, blunderbusses, arquebusses and pistols.

'Then where will it end, Yetaxa?' Autloc's voice quavered.

'In total destruction,' Barbara replied softly. 'Your civilisation will pass forever from this land.'

'You prophesy our doom.' Autloc's hands quivered in despair.

Barbara stood silently beside the throne and waited.

'Let me think on these words, great Spirit,' he said finally, bowed to her and hurried from the temple.

Barbara watched him leave. What are you playing at Barbara Wright? she asked herself. Still trying to meddle with history? You know it can't be done, didn't the Doctor tell you, didn't you ignore him, and fail? So what are you doing quoting facts and statistics out of history books and causing enormous distress to the only Aztec ally you have? She felt ashamed and suddenly very tired. She left the temple and went down to the antechamber to rest.

7

No Holds Barred

The High Priests met on the stairs and Autloc related word for word all that Barbara had told him.

'So she prophesies our doom,' Tlotoxl sneered. 'Without doubt to avert her own.' He jabbed a finger at Autloc. 'I tell you she is not Yetaxa, she is a false God.'

'I do not know it,' Autloc replied firmly.

'Question her again and again and again, then you will learn I speak the truth.'

They heard the Doctor puffing his way up the stairs.

'The old man,' Tlotoxl said, 'let us withdraw.'

They hid in the shadows of an alcove and watched the Doctor as he muttered that he was too old for this sort of thing and continued climbing up the stairs to the antechamber where Barbara was resting.

She started as he came in. 'Doctor, go away,' but he flopped onto a couch instead. 'No one's allowed to see me.'

'Nonsense,' the Doctor gasped, 'the guards didn't stop me.' He waved an arm vaguely towards the door. 'And besides, I'm supposed to be your aged servant.' There was a hint of sarcasm in his voice which Barbara decided to ignore.

'Didn't Tlotoxl warn you that during my questioning none of you are allowed up here?'

'No,' the Doctor stood up wearily. 'All right, I'll go as soon as I've told you that I'll know how to get into the tomb by tonight.'

Barbara was relieved. 'I won't be sorry,' she said.

'All I had to do was make sure that the warrior grandson of the man who built this temple wins a fight at sunset,' the Doctor confided with a wink.

'But that's Ixta,' Barbara cried, 'Ian's rival for command, and it's to be a fight to the death, Tlotoxl told me so.'

The Doctor was alarmed. 'I must warn Chesterton,' he said and went to the antechamber door. He opened it, but the way was barred by two guards with Tlotoxl and Autloc.

'Take him,' Tlotoxl commanded, 'he has transgressed the law.'

The guards seized the Doctor's arms and led him away as he protested in vain. Tlotoxl followed them. Autloc remained and Barbara looked at him angrily.

'They had no right to arrest my aged servant.'

'As the High Priest of Sacrifice observed, he has . . .'

Barbara cut him of with a chopping motion of her hand. 'No one told him! He didn't know!'

Autloc frowned. 'If that is so then to hold him prisoner is unjust. I shall obtain his release.'

'I thank you, Autloc.'

The High Priest bowed and turned to leave the antechamber.

'Wait,' Barbara said suddenly, 'There is to be a contest between my servant, Ian, and the chosen warrior, Ixta. I forbid it.'

Autloc looked at her uncomfortably. 'Great Spirit, the contest cannot be avoided. Only one of them may command our armies.'

'Then let it be Ixta.'

Autloc was shocked. 'You deny your servant honour?' he asked.

Barbara shook her head and said that the contest was ill-timed, that Ixta had been in training for many months. Autloc protested that he had seen Ian defeat Ixta with his thumb and, besides, the combat would not be mortal.

'See that it remains so,' Barbara commanded.

'Yetaxa has spoken,' Autloc replied and bowed again.

Ian and Ixta faced each other across the courtyard. They wore loin-cloths and sandals. Tonila and the Perfect Victim stood against one wall. The Perfect Victim held two cudgels. He looked at Ixta, then at Ian, both of whom nodded. The Perfect Victim raised the cudgels above his head.

'Let the contest begin,' he called, striking the cudgels together.

Ian and Ixta circled each other warily, which in Ixta's case was a mistake as Ian suddenly lunged at him. Ixta reached out to grab Ian's arms, but Ian broke the attempted hold by swinging his arms in a full circle and at the same time his right foot shot behind Ixta's left ankle and jerked him off balance. Ixta staggered back and Ian moved in, grabbing the Chosen Warrior by one arm, then turning away abruptly to go for a shoulder throw. Ixta had sense enough to realise that if he tried to resist his arm would break. He hit the ground face down in front of Ian who didn't release his arm but, holding it in a handlock, began kneading Ixta's muscle with his other fist. Both Tonila and the Perfect Victim were impressed but Ixta wanted to cry out in fury as he felt the strength draining away from his arm. He knew that with an arm useless he had already lost the contest. Somehow he had to break Ian's hold and reach the thorn which he had carefully placed beside the door to his quarters.

Then Ian made his mistake. Knowing Ixta's arm was completely weakened, he released his handhold and stepped back. Using his good arm and under Ian's watchful eyes, Ixta rose to his knees and massaged his useless arm. At that moment Tlotoxl, Autloc and the Doctor came into the courtyard.

'Don't let him scratch you, Chesterton,' the Doctor shouted immediately. Ian was puzzled and looked at the Doctor.

'Scratch me?' he asked. The distraction gave Ixta enough time to scramble to his feet, race to the door, grab the thorn and throw himself at Ian who easily blocked the attack but not before the thorn had been drawn across the inside of his wrist.

'Use stealth, use cunning you said,' Ixta was jubilant. 'You defeated me with your thumb, I have defeated you with the thorn of the maguey cactus.'

'Plus a sleep-inducing herb,' the Doctor protested as Ixta threw away the thorn. Ian knew that to win he had to do it quickly. He also realised that the more energy he expended, the harder his heart would pump and the faster the drug would circulate through his system. He needed a submission hammerlock, but Ixta was keeping his distance, dancing out of the way, waiting.

'Stop this childish nonsense, Tlotoxl,' the Doctor demanded, 'stop it.'

Tlotoxl had victory in his eyes as he looked at the Doctor. 'No.'

'But I gave Ixta the thorn,' the Doctor protested.

'Then you should rejoice,' Tlotoxl replied.' Ixta will win.'

'Autloc, stop it,' the Doctor pleaded, 'the contest is unfair.'

'I cannot.' Autloc was embarrassed. 'The Perfect Victim desired this contest and only the High Priest of Sacrifice, who commands here, can stop it.'

'Let it continue,' the Perfect Victim requested. Tlotoxl bowed.

'And to the death, Ixta, to the death,' he called ecstatically.

Ixta bent down to pick up one of the studded cudgels. This is my last chance, Ian thought, and rushed at the Chosen Warrior. Once again he caught Ixta off balance and pushed him to his knees. Knowing he no longer had the strength for the submission hold, Ian clamped on a half-nelson and went for the pressure point again with his thumb. But his head was beginning to swim, his eyes blurring and his strength ebbing away. Ixta threw him off. Ian rolled over and stood up groggily while Ixta picked up the second cudgel and handed it cautiously to him.

'I have but one arm but soon you will sleep,' Ixta smiled at Ian, 'forever, and I shall command our armies.' He swung his cudgel at Ian's head. Ian saw it coming and fended off the blow, but it sent him reeling.

'Destroy him, Ixta,' Tlotoxl was triumphant.

'Yetaxa forbade it,' Autloc replied.

'A false God forbids it,' Tlotoxl sneered, and turned back to Ixta. 'Destroy him.'

Ian warded off the repeated blows as best he could, but he knew he had only seconds to live. And then he heard Barbara's voice.

'Stop!' she commanded as she stood at the entrance to the courtyard. Ixta lowered his cudgel, Ian reeling did the same. Tlotoxl turned to Barbara, with venom in his voice.

'Your place is in the temple.'

'Even though I am a false God? No, Tlotoxl, I am loyal to those who serve me.'

Tlotoxl looked at her with loathing and then turned to Ixta. 'Execute him,' he cried out exultantly, then looked at Barbara. 'If you are Yetaxa – save him,' pointing to Ian as Ixta raised the cudgel.

Ian barely saw the movement, but he succeeded in blocking the blow, knowing that the next one would bury the studs in his brain. Ixta raised the cudgel to strike but before he could bring it down Barbara held Tlotoxl from behind, the razor-sharp edge of an obsidian knife against his throat.

'As dies my servant, so dies your High Priest of Sacrifice.'

Everyone froze. It was no idle threat and they all knew it, Tlotoxl included. He looked at Ixta and shook his head slowly, carefully. Ixta lowered the cudgel. 'Now, both of you, put them to one side,' Barbara ordered, still keeping the knife at Tlotoxl's throat.

Ian dropped his cudgel and Ixta laid his on the ground. Tonila waddled over and picked them up, then gave them to the Perfect Victim who struck them over his head.

'Neither of the Chosen Warriors may claim a victory,' he announced.

Barbara came from behind Tlotoxl to face him but she still had the knife in her hand.

'I did as you commanded. Now you must obey me.'

Tlotoxl closed his eyes.

'My servants shall not be punished.'

'So be it,' Tlotoxl replied almost inaudibly, as Ian slid to the ground and slept.

Several minutes later the High Priest of Sacrifice stood with Ixta in his quarters. The Chosen Warrior was suffering from pins and needles in his hand as his blood circulation was restored and his arm came gradually back to life.

'With my bare hands I cannot defeat him,' he admitted ruefully, but added that he was determined to command their armies.

'So you shall,' Tlotoxl spoke soothingly and opened his right hand. Lying in the palm was the cactus thorn which Tlotoxl had picked up from the ground. 'Why did the old man give you this to win a victory?'

'It was a trick,' Ixta smiled. 'He did not know the contest was with Ian and he promised to help me if I told him the secrets of my father's father's work.'

'What secrets?' Tlotoxl was intrigued.

'How the tomb of Yetaxa may be entered,' Ixta flexed his arm, opening and closing his hand.

'I must question him about it.' Tlotoxl placed the thorn

on the table.

'He was at my mercy.' Ixta was suddenly tense with frustration.

'And shall be again,' the High Priest promised before he limped away.

8

Cups of Cocoa

Barbara sat on the throne in the temple and looked down at the worried High Priest of Knowledge who stood in front of her.

'Tlotoxl was humiliated. He will not forget, nor will he forgive,' he warned her.

Barbara shrugged. 'I did as he commanded.'

'But not as he expected.'

'What did he want, a miracle?' She smiled at Autloc.

'We all awaited one,' he confessed.

Barbara stood and stepped down to the temple floor. 'Why should I use divine powers when human ability will suffice?' she asked sweetly.

Autloc could not resist a twitch of a grin. 'Yetaxa has spoken,' he tried to keep his tone of voice solemn.

Barbara walked towards the terrace and the sacrificial altar. A few paces short of it, she stopped and turned back to face the High Priest. 'Have you thought about my prophesy?'

'On little else. And it is true that if we defy the will of the Gods we shall be destroyed.'

'When Quetzecoatl reigned supreme as the Sun God

was there human sacrifice?'

'No, only after his banishment was blood demanded.'

'By Huitzilipochtli, the dark God of the Sun.' Barbara put her hand around the bracelet on her wrist. 'What sacrifice did Quetzecoatl demand?'

'A bird, a fish, a serpent, none other.'

'Why should that have been?'

'He so dearly loved his people he wished no harm to anyone,' Autloc explained.

'Is not a return of Quetzecoatl possible?'

'Only a God can banish a God. We mortals can do nothing.'

'And were Quetzecoatl to send you a messenger?' Barbara took her hand off the bracelet.

Autloc glanced at it and looked away. 'I serve Huitzilipochtli,' he said quietly, 'this is his temple.'

'Then where must Quetzecoatl seek his servants?'

Autloc remained silent and Barbara shifted tack. 'When is to be the next sacrifice?' she asked.

'Three days from this day,'Autloc replied, 'the moon will pass before the sun when it is at its zenith and all will be in darkness.'

'So there's to be an eclipse and Tlotoxl will offer a human heart.'

'The Perfect Victim's.'

'And the sun will shine again!' Barbara stamped her sandalled foot angrily. 'As the High Priest of Knowledge, you must know that the moon will pass across the sun and continue on its celestial voyage.'

'Unless Huitzilipochtli, the Sun God, the Supreme God, withdraws his favour from us.' Autloc was adamant.

'Am I not a God?' Barbara heard herself say with a shock. There was no turning back for her now. 'Support me, Autloc,' she pleaded, 'the High Priest of Sacrifice won't dare defy us both.'

Autloc bent his head and touched his lips with the posy he held. A full minute passed in silence, then he raised his head and looked at Barbara. 'If you come as Quetzecoatl's messenger and I take your course, there is no way back for me. So in all humility I entreat you not to deceive me nor prove false to me.'

Barbara's appearance remained serene but her heart ached and she was in mental anguish.

Tlotoxl sidled up to the Doctor, who was sitting disconsolately in the garden.

'What manner of servant are you?' the High Priest asked.

'Oh, go away,' the Doctor snapped, but Tlotoxl sat down beside him.

'I am curious about you,' he said. 'First you try to secure a victory for Ixta.'

'He cheated me,' the Doctor replied hotly.

Tlotoxl looked sideways at the Doctor.

'I am faithful to my friends,' the Doctor insisted.

'Yet you deceive Yetaxa.'

'Not at all,' the Doctor was indignant.

'You are trying to enter the tomb without Yetaxa's knowledge,' the High Priest studied the edge of his obsidian knife. 'What is it you want from there?'

'What is it you want from me?' the Doctor countered.

'But one thing,' Tlotoxl held up the knife, 'proof that she is a false God.'

'Then open the tomb.'

'That cannot be achieved.'

'Can't it?' the Doctor raised an eyebrow. 'Talk to your Chosen Warrior. He has a drawing.'

Tlotoxl stared with glinting black eyes at the Doctor. 'In whose service are you?' he asked.

The Doctor took the knife from Tlotoxl and touched both edges with his thumb, then handed the weapon back to him. 'In the service of truth,' the Doctor replied, a touch pompously, 'and if you help me, you'll also find it.'

When Ian awoke he was lying on the straw mattress in the bedroom of his quarters, but he was not alone. Standing over him was a smiling Ixta with a short sword in his hand. Ian struggled to sit up so that he could, at least, try to defend himself.

'Do not be afraid of me, Ian,' Ixta laughed. 'Now that I can defeat you openly, I have no need to destroy you in secret.'

'Whatever it was you scratched me with, beat me,' Ian mumbled and rubbed his temples with his fingers trying to clear the cobwebs from his brain.

'Did you not say "use stealth, surprise your enemy"?' Ixta was enjoying himself.

'True,' Ian admitted.

'And did I not do those things?' Ixta laughed again.

Ian agreed that he had.

'A thorn, the sap of a plant and Yetaxa's aged servant,' Ixta added.

Ian looked up sharply. 'The Doctor helped you?'

Ixta nodded and remarked that Ian's friends made strange allies.

Ian stood up gingerly. 'Did the Doctor know you were to fight me?' he asked.

Ixta shook his head and admitted that he didn't.

Ian felt dizzy. 'I need some fresh air.' He staggered towards the living area and the door of his quarters.

'Let me help you.' Ixta took his arm. 'Now that I have proved I will be the victor, we can be friends. For the little time that is left to you to live,' he added almost as an afterthought.

'Oh, I'm going to die, am I?' Ian's voice expressed no surprise.

'Yes, Ian.' Ixta sounded enthusiastic at the prospect. 'Next time we fight, I shall not fail to kill you.'

'It's always worth knowing in advance,' Ian remarked as he went into the courtyard and leaned against the wall beside the open door. He shut his eyes and breathed deeply several times. When he opened them, Tlotoxl and Tonila were crossing the courtyard.

'I see your strength has been restored to you,' Tlotoxl sneered.

'Don't tell me you've become my friend as well,' Ian joked, and saw the flash of hatred in the High Priest's eyes before Tlotoxl turned abruptly to Ixta.

'I have need of the drawing,' he said.

'The one I promised to the aged servant?' Ixta roared with laughter when Tlotoxl nodded. 'It doesn't exist. The secret of the tomb disappeared with my father.'

'But your father's father must have set it down,' Tlotoxl sounded anxious.

Ian listened to the conversation with great interest.

'No. He told it to my father, who thought to do so. But one evening he went for a walk in the garden and was never seen again.'

'I recall his disappearance.' Tlotoxl was brusque.

So that's why the Doctor helped you, Ian thought, he hoped to have a design plan of the tomb. Then another thought occurred to Ian: neither Ixta nor Tlotoxl had used the word 'died' when they talked about his father. They had used the word 'disappeared', and Ixta had referred to the garden. This set Ian speculating.

Ignoring Ian, the High Priest of Sacrifice and Tonila took their leave of Ixta and limped and waddled towards the gate way to the courtyard.

Tlotoxl began to speak. 'You are well versed in these

matters, Tonila,' Ian overheard him say, 'so you shall help me to defeat the false . . .' Then they were out of earshot, but Ian was convinced the sentence had ended 'God Yetaxa'.

He was right and Tonila was outraged at Tlotoxl's suggestion. 'No, I cannot obey your bidding, I will not.' He gesticulated wildly. 'Destroy a God and we destroy ourselves.'

Tlotoxl pointed out that true Gods were immortal and that mere flesh and blood, as they both were, could not destroy them. Tonila looked at him warily and asked in what way Tlotoxl required his services.

'Your knowledge of poisons.'

Tonila was horrified.

'Such a test, a poisoned draught, would prove her divinity. If she dies, she is false; if she lives, then she is indeed the spirit of Yetaxa returned.'

Tonila's throat dried as Tlotoxl looked at him slyly. 'Would you deny yourself the honour – more, the glory – of witnessing a God proven before your eyes?'

Tonila ran his tongue around his mouth seeking saliva to ease his throat. He swallowed. 'I shall prepare a mixture,' he said, 'then you and I and Autloc shall test Yetaxa.'

'Autloc? I think not,' Tlotoxl snapped.

'Why not?'

Tlotoxl despised Tonila's naivety, but his voice was quiet and reasonable as he argued that Autloc's mind was set that Yetaxa was a true God and he would forbid the test. 'No, you and I shall do this thing and for once the High Priest of Knowledge shall be in ignorance.' He glanced at Tonila and almost managed a thin smile.

At the same time, the High Priest of Knowledge was basking in Cameca's radiant smile as they walked along a path in the garden.

'Such happiness, Cameca, outshines the sun,' he remarked.

'And with good fortune may outlast it,' Cameca replied softly.

'What brings you such joy?'

Cameca looked around the garden and saw the Doctor studying a carved coiled snake on one of the stones of the back wall of the garden. Cameca raised her hand and pointed to him. A small leather bag hung from a cord around her wrist. Autloc smiled.

'I am grateful to Yetaxa's aged servant,' he said, and noticing the bag, asked if Cameca was carrying cocoa beans to barter with.

She shook her head. 'I have already been to the market and bought food,' she replied.

Autloc touched the bag. 'Then these are to prepare a drink.'

Cameca lowered her eyes. 'Only the Gods may know,' she replied coyly.

'Ah,' Autloc murmured, and observed that all mortals lived in hope.

'He is a gentle companion and most dear to me,' Cameca admitted.

'Are these then for a love potion?' Autloc asked in mock surprise.

'That would be too bold,' Cameca blushed, 'rather should he show his love for me.'

'You wish him to prepare it.'

'Yes.'

Autloc looked from her to the Doctor and back to Cameca again. 'May the Gods favour your desires,' he said gently and walked away.

Cameca went over to the Doctor and greeted him.

The Doctor half-replaced the bougainvillea over the carved stone and turned to face her. 'My dear Cameca, how nice it is to see you again.' He took her hand. 'The garden is a lonely place without you.'

She glanced at the wall. 'When one's interest is held, loneliness does not exist.'

The Doctor followed her eye-line to the carving partly hidden behind the flowered trellis. 'I was looking at it – hadn't noticed it before,' he explained.

'The coiled serpent of Yetaxa. In almost every building homage is paid to the High Priest with that symbol.' Cameca drew aside the bougainvillea and snagged her bag on the trellis. As she pulled it free some of the cocoa beans fell onto the ground.

The Doctor began picking them up. 'Cocoa beans,' he exclaimed.

'We use them for barter for our daily needs,' Cameca replied.

'What an excellent idea, a currency you can drink,' the Doctor proclaimed. 'Delicious!'

'Do you know our customs?' Cameca asked timidly as the Doctor dropped the beans one by one back into her bag.

'Why, yes, my dear, of course,' the Doctor replied, looking about him to make sure he hadn't overlooked a bean.

'The drinking of cocoa has its own very special meaning,' Cameca ventured and the Doctor wholeheartedly agreed with her.

'It's a rare delight and we shall take a cup together.'

'Are you certain?'

The Doctor missed her shyness. 'Yes, yes, quite,' he replied, 'now give me the beans and I'll go to the kitchen and brew some up.'

'You insist?' Cameca was hesitant.

'I do. I insist as a token of my esteem.'

Cameca's face lit up as she gave the Doctor the bag of

beans. 'The Gods are smiling favour through your eyes, may it always be so,' she said. 'My dear Doctor, I accept with all my heart.'

'Now, don't go away, my dear,' the Doctor cautioned her, 'I'll be back.'

Clutching the bag of cocoa beans, he marched off to the small kitchen in one corner of the garden where the old people could take a drink of cool fresh water, or prepare a corn pancake with honey, or a goblet of hot cocoa, over the wood fire. The Doctor found the mortar and pestle, and ground sufficient beans for two goblets. He sang quietly to himself. It had been a long time since he had drunk cocoa and he was looking forward to it. He put the powder equally into the two goblets, added hot water, and sweetened them both with honey.

Proudly he returned to the bench where Cameca sat and handed her a goblet before sitting down beside her.

'Happy days, my dear.' He chinked his goblet against hers in a toast.

Cameca's eyes were dewy. 'The happiest of my life, dear heart,' she replied and they sipped their cocoas. 'Was ever such a potion brewed? In bliss is quenched my thirsty heart.'

'Very prettily put, my dear,' the Doctor muttered approvingly.

Cameca turned to him and kissed him on both cheeks. 'Oh, sweet, favoured man, you have declared your love for me,' she said, 'and I acknowledge and accept your gentle proposal.'

The Doctor found the next sip of cocoa infinitely more difficult to swallow.

9

Bride of Sacrifice

Ian went up the temple stairs two at a time. He wore his Chosen Warrior's loin-cloth and embroidered cloak, as well as a plumed battle-mask in hammered silver which concealed the upper half of his face. The temple guards saluted him and one drew back the brocade curtain to let him pass.

Barbara was standing on the terrace looking down at the city. She was startled when Ian came towards her, not certain for a moment whether it was him or Ixta. Ian lifted his mask and Barbara sighed with relief before frowning. 'You shouldn't be up here. It's too dangerous,' she said anxiously.

Ian dismissed her fears with a downward wave of his hand and remarked lightly that, for all the guards knew, he could just as easily have been Ixta.

Barbara wasn't convinced. 'I still think it was reckless of you.'

Ian led her to the back of the temple behind the throne. 'I came here to warn you,' he confided.

'About what?'

'That's the problem, I don't know. But I'm convinced that Tlotoxl and Tonila are cooking up something against you.'

Barbara was surprised. 'Tonila? I didn't realise he was on Tlotoxl's side. Our High Priest of Sacrifice seems to have the knack of bringing people round to his way of thinking,' she added ruefully.

'That's where you're wrong, Barbara,' Ian replied. 'They're all on Tlotoxl's side.'

'What about Autloc?' she asked.

'What about him?' Ian shrugged. 'He's reasonable, cultured, civilised in himself, but he goes along with Tlotoxl. You saved my life, Barbara, not Autloc. He would have let me die.'

'I'm not so sure that he would now.' She did her best to sound convincing as she told Ian about her last conversation with the High Priest of Knowledge.

Ian shook his head. 'Cometh the crunch, Barbara, he'll behave like an Aztec.' Ian was adamant. 'You can't fight a whole way of life.'

Barbara turned away. 'First from the Doctor, now from you,' she laughed mirthlessly. 'But there's such nobility in them,' she protested, 'that I want to do something to save them from destruction.'

'There's only one thing to be done,' Ian said quietly to her back, 'get back into that tomb and leave them alone.'

Barbara heard faint footsteps on the stairs. 'Someone's coming up,' she whispered, 'hide.'

Ian dashed to the curtain behind which he and Ixta had held the Rain God victim. He ducked into the alcove, holding one slit of the curtain open with a finger so that he could see Barbara, who had taken her place on the throne. He heard Tlotoxl's shuffling gait as he limped over to the throne with Tonila at his side, holding a goblet.

'We greet Yetaxa,' Tlotoxl said ingratiatingly.

'What do you want?' Barbara asked coldly.

Tlotoxl gestured to Tonila and himself. 'We come

before the Great Spirit in all humility,' and they both bowed.

'Quiet words do you credit.' Barbara's eyes and mind were alert for any indication of danger.

Tlotoxl stretched out his arm in a gesture of despair. 'Have we not both spoken harsh words and had dark thoughts?' He went on to state that he was now convinced of her divinity and wished to make amends.

Tonila echoed Tlotoxl by begging Yetaxa not to punish the High Priest for his misgivings.

'This draught is symbolic of the blood of Huitzil-ipochtli.' Tlotoxl took the goblet from Tonila and held it up in front of Barbara. 'Let us share it in reverence.'

Barbara took the goblet from him and raised it to her lips. Behind the curtain Ian held his breath and tensed his muscles, ready to dash out to knock the goblet from her hands before she drank. Tlotoxl and Tonila watched her intently.

Then, she hesitated, smiled and held out the goblet to the High Priest. 'If you now acknowledge my divinity, then first both of you must drink in reverence to me,' she shot a quick glance at Tonila who averted his eyes, 'and then I shall drink in reverence to Huitzilipochtli for us all.' She stood and thrust the goblet at him. 'Drink,' she commanded.

The High Priest took a step backwards. Barbara came down from the dais and turned to Tonila. 'You'll sip it in reverence to me, won't you?'

The balding, pudgy little priest shook his head and edged his way towards the curtained entrance to the temple. Holding the goblet at arm's length, Barbara went with him. As he reached the curtain Barbara looked at him icily. 'You defile this temple. Get out of my sight.' She threw down the goblet, which smashed at his feet, and Tonila fled.

Barbara turned back to face Tlotoxl who looked at her apprehensively. 'Well?' Her voice was expressionless.

'We meant only to test you.'

'With poison.' Still she betrayed no emotion.

'Yetaxa would have lived as true Gods are immortal.'

'Well, I would have died.'

Tlotoxl's eyes widened in triumph.

'I am not Yetaxa.'

He pointed at her. 'False! You are a false God. As I have known since first I saw you.'

'And who will believe you?' Barbara's eyes hardened. 'I warn you, Tlotoxl. Say one word against me to the people and I shall have them destroy you. Now, go.'

The High Priest of Sacrifice stared malevolently at her for a few seconds. Barbara met his eyes with a steady gaze, then he muttered the word 'false' again, and limped from the temple.

As soon as he was gone Barbara began to tremble. Ian came quickly from behind the curtain and put his arms around her. Barbara closed her eyes. 'W-w-we m-m-must get away, Ian,' she stammered, 'I can't p-pl-play this r-r-role much lon-longer.'

'We will, Barbara, we will,' he reassured her, but he didn't know how they would do it.

It was early afternoon. The two High Priests and Tonila had eaten their mid-day meal of roast pheasant, hot spicy pancakes, and fruit, all of which had been prepared by the women who served in the temple. The three of them sat on cushions around the table rinsing their hands in the finger bowls which had been placed in front of them.

'What progress do our pupils make at the seminary, Tonila?' Autloc dabbed his mouth with a dampened corner of his napkin.

'All are diligent in their studies,' Tonila replied.

'And Yetaxa's handmaiden?' Autloc asked.

Tonila raised his arms. 'Her intelligence far exceeds that of the others. And she has knowledge of things known only to the Priests,' he added, clearly impressed.

'But are you surprised? She also serves the Gods,' Autloc reminded him.

'Other Gods than ours,' Tlotoxl growled.

Autloc sighed and asked when the High Priest of Sacrifice would cease to doubt Yetaxa's divinity.

'Never, for I know she is false,' he snapped, and was on the point of telling Autloc about the poison but realised that they had tried to give it to her without his knowldge. 'She has come amongst us, intent on destroying us.' He slammed his fist onto the table.

'Or saving us,' Autloc replied quietly as he stood up and went to his cell to rest.

Tlotoxl flicked crumbs of food off the table. 'Do you share Autloc's conviction?' he asked Tonila.

'I do not know to whom I should listen.' Tonila nervously remembered the goblet exploding, splashing the poisoned draught over his feet.

'She is false, she told me so herself,' Tlotoxl said but saw the doubt in Tonila's eyes. 'And when I have the proof you will hear only my voice which will be like thunder in the sky.' He cleaned his fingernails with the tip of a knife. 'But where is my proof, how shall I obtain it? She is very clever.' He put down the knife and studied his nails, then looked at Tonila. 'The handmaiden, alone in the seminary, tell me about her.'

Tonila shifted uncomfortably on his cushion. 'She is, as I have said, very intelligent but self-willed.'

'In what way?' Tlotoxl leaned across the table.

'One day, in the presence of the High Priest of Knowledge and myself, she said she would only marry someone of her own choosing.'

'She would not be wed by arrangement, nor for honour?'

Tonila shook his head. 'On this she was firm. She would choose her husband.' A plan had already formulated in Tlotoxl's mind. 'Then we must find a suitable one for her, Tonila,' he said briskly and put a forefinger to his lips. 'The false God's weakness lies not in herself but in her servants,' he observed as he picked up the knife and stuck it into the table.

A prospective husband was the last thought in Susan's mind as she stood, bored almost to tears, at the entrance to her cell, looking out onto the cloister. Behind her was Autloc, the ever-present posy in his hand.

'In the annals of Cuauhtitlan there is the myth of the five suns in the sky,' he intoned. 'Name them.' Susan took a breath and reeled them off in a monotone.

'The first was known as Four-Tiger, the second the sun of Air, the third the sun of Fire and Rain, the fourth the sun of Water and, finally, the present one, the sun of Man.'

Autloc was delighted. 'Excellent, Susan, excellent.'

Susan resigned herself to the next question but it was never posed. Suddenly Tonila and the Perfect Victim were standing beside the doorway.

'I greet you, Autloc,' Tonila said.

The High Priest's face fell when he saw the Perfect Victim.

'As I do also,' the young man said, smiling at Susan.

'You honour us with your visit,' Autloc replied, 'how may we serve you?'

'It is my wish to look at her.'

Susan was puzzled, Autloc troubled and Tonila amused.

'Do you know who she is?' Autloc asked.

The Perfect Victim smiled. 'Does she know who I am?'

'No.'

'Then tell her.'

'In two days, when the sun is at its zenith, darkness will descend upon the land,' Autloc said.

'All great Huitzilipochtli's light hidden from our eyes,' Tonila added mystically.

'You mean it'll be a total eclipse.' Susan was enthusiastic and remarked that, although she had seen several partial eclipses, she had never seen one where the sun was completely hidden by the moon. 'It'll be interesting to watch.'

Autloc shifted uneasily. 'At the moment when all is in darkness, a human sacrifice will be offered to the Sun God and this young man . . .'

Susan's hands flew to her face. '. . . is to be the victim!' she blurted out in horror. 'But that's revolting.'

The young man looked at her uncomprehendingly. 'What greater honour is there for me than to be chosen as the Perfect Victim and to join the Gods?' His voice rang with pride. Then he announced he would take Susan as his bride.

She gaped at him in utter incredulity before giving vent to her feelings. 'Bride!' She pointed at him. 'He thinks I'll marry him? Well, if he's mad enough to let himself be sacrificed because of a stupid eclipse I suppose he's mad enough to believe anything.'

Tonila protested that since the young man had been chosen as the Perfect Victim, all his desires were granted. 'That does not include me!' Susan was furious. 'Let him die if he wants to, but don't expect me to marry him.'

'It is the Aztec law, Susan,' Autloc chided her.

'Then your law is barbaric and I won't obey it. I won't!' Susan shouted. 'You're monsters, all of you are monsters!' She ran from the cell onto the cloister.

Tonila looked at Autloc. 'She has broken the law,' he said, 'it must be reported to Tlotoxl.'

'Let her be severely punished for denying me,' the Perfect Victim added.

Autloc looked from one to the other. 'So be it,' he murmured.

With tears streaming down her cheeks, Susan ran half-way around the cloister before collapsing against a pillar.

'Grandfather, grandfather,' she sobbed, 'please, help me.'

10

Offence and Retribution

It was evening and the air in the garden was heavily scented as the Doctor, lost in his thoughts, walked along a path, his hands clutched behind his back. There had to be another way into the tomb, he reasoned, for how else could the counterbalanced wall have been set in place? It would have required builders both in the tomb and outside in the temple. He presumed that the temple, and consequently the tomb, had been built before Yetaxa's death as the pyramid must have taken a decade to construct and that, the Doctor considered, was a long time to keep a corpse hanging around waiting to be laid to rest. So, when Yetaxa died someone, Ixta's grandfather perhaps, had to open up the wall from inside the tomb. Ergo, there had to be a secret entrance to steps leading up to a trapdoor, most likely, and now possibly sealed, in the floor of the tomb.

The Doctor sighed and sniffed the perfumed air without appreciating it. How would the trapdoor be sealed? he asked himself. Closed, it would be seated on a flange which, once Yetaxa's body was placed in the tomb, could have been lined with terracotta, a mixture of sand and clay, that would harden like a brick when heated. Yes, that must be the answer, the Doctor decided and then wondered how much force would be required to break the seal. A hammer, a chisel and Chesterton's biceps would suffice, he concluded. All that now remained was to locate the secret entrance to the steps and that, he realised dejectedly, could be almost anywhere. But where would be the likeliest place?

'Doctor,' Cameca's voice broke his train of thought. Irritated, he saw her coming along the path towards him. 'My dear, I am glad to find you alone as I have a gift for you.'

'How very kind,' the Doctor mumbled, wondering if it were more cocoa beans. Instead, she gave him a beautiful jade brooch with an eagle and, separately, a coiled snake carved on it.

He was taken aback. 'Dear lady, I cannot possibly accept such a . . .' he began but stopped when Cameca said the gift signified her love for him. The Doctor swallowed. 'I shall treasure it always.'

'I am pleased, though it is yours by right.'

The Doctor was puzzled. 'Why do you say that?' he asked.

'It came from Yetaxa's tomb.'

The Doctor was dumbfounded. 'From where?'

'The tomb. See, it has Yetaxa's sign on it,' she pointed to the snake, 'the coiled serpent.'

'But that is the emblem of the Aztec nation,' the Doctor said.

'That is so,' Cameca replied, 'only the serpent is held either in the eagle's beak or its claws. Yetaxa's sign of the coiled serpent is separate from the eagle.'

The Doctor turned the brooch over in his hands. 'It is quite magnificent.' He smiled at her and asked casually how she had come by it.

Cameca blushed. 'Though married, Ixta's father fell in love with me. I did what I could to discourage his advances. But he insisted that I accept the brooch, which he gave to me seven days before he disappeared.'

'Disappeared?'

'Yes, here, in this garden,' Cameca replied, 'he was never seen again.' She dismissed the topic with a gesture of her hand. 'But it was a long time ago and now I look forward to a life of bliss with you.'

'And I with you, my dear,' the Doctor said absently, his mind on other matters.

'Peace and contentment,' Cameca reflected.

'Serenity,' the Doctor echoed.

'We shall have a garden of our own,' she announced.

The Doctor's eyes lit up. 'Yes, of course,' he agreed, 'a garden of our own.' And his eyes travelled to the wall and the stone with the coiled snake carved on it.

As soon as he decently could the Doctor took his leave of Cameca and hurried to the barracks. When the Doctor burst into his quarters, Ian was desperately trying to think of something constructive he could do to put them safely back on board the TARDIS and get them on their way.

'Eureka, Chesterton, I have it!' the Doctor exclaimed,

and then hesitated, 'or at least I think I have.'

'What?' Ian asked, taken aback.

The Doctor held the brooch in the palm of his right hand and poked it with his left forefinger. 'This came from Yetaxa's tomb. And who took it?' he demanded without waiting for an answer. 'His father!' He pointed dramatically at Ixta's quarters on the other side of the courtyard and then poked the brooch again. 'So there's the proof that a secret way into the tomb exists and Ixta's father knew about it.' The Doctor looked about him conspiratorily and moved closer to Ian. 'But what is much more important, Chesterton, my dear boy, is that I believe I know where it is.' His voice was little more than an urgent whisper. 'Underneath the garden is an irrigation tunnel used for watering the flowers, and in the back wall is a stone with a coiled snake – Yetaxa's sign – carved on it. I'm certain that the stone can be removed to reveal a way into the tunnel. I'm convinced that under the temple wall there will be a flight of stairs leading up to the tomb.' The Doctor's eyes darted here and there in search of a possible eavesdropper before he continued. 'Tonight, Chesterton, tonight, once Ixta is asleep, come to the garden where I shall be waiting for you.'

'All right, Doctor, I'll be there,' Ian said.

'Good fellow,' the Doctor replied and slapped him on the back.

'How did you get hold of this?' Ian asked, tapping the brooch.

The Doctor cleared his throat. 'My fiancée gave it to me as a present.'

'I see,' Ian replied before it registered. 'Your what?' he choked.

'I made some cocoa and became engaged to Cameca.'

Ian began to chuckle.

'It's no laughing matter, Chesterton.'

Ian tried to keep a straight face.

'And the sooner we're away from here, the better.'

'Yes, Doctor,' Ian managed to reply, his shoulders shaking. 'I'll be there tonight.'

The Doctor turned to leave.

'Oh, and by the way, Doctor, congratulations,' he said and doubled up.

The Doctor stormed off. From his quarters Ixta watched him go.

Barbara was in the antechamber when a guard announced that the High Priest of Sacrifice and the Priest of Knowledge awaited her in the temple. Her defences came up instinctively. 'Say that I shall receive them presently,' she said.

The guard bowed and withdrew.

Barbara considered her strategy. Should she listen to them first and then riposte as best she could, or should she go directly on the attack? She placed the plumed crown on her head and decided on the latter course of action. When she reached the temple, she ignored them until she sat upon the throne.

'Why do you attend me?' Her voice was glacial.

Tlotoxl kept his eyes fixed on her while Tonila looked down at his posy and shuffled his feet. 'There is a matter we would place before you, Great Spirit,' he burbled.

Barbara raised one eyebrow. 'You wish the Gods to favour the Priest of Knowledge with their good opinions?'

'Their advice,' Tonila conceded.

'Yet you sin against them with your test of poison,' Barbara snapped as Tonila studied his posy even more intently.

'Let us talk of this other matter,' Tlotoxl cajoled.

'Be quiet.' It was like a whiplash across his back, but

he gritted his teeth and contained his fury.

Barbara looked back at Tonila. 'Your offence against the Gods is forgiven. Now, what would you discuss?'

'The punishment for one who talks out against our teachings and defies our laws.' Barbara realised that this time it was a verbal trap Tlotoxl was trying to spring.

'Was this spoken in public?' she asked cautiously.

'Yes, Great Spirit, and after being duly warned,' Tonila emphasised.

'Were there witnesses to the warning?' One step at a time, she thought.

'Autloc and myself.'

'What was the offence?' Barbara was concerned that Autloc was involved and curious to know why he wasn't with them.

'Denying a desire of the Perfect Victim.'

'Be specific, Tonila. What was his wish?' Like the poisoned draught, she guessed this interview was being conducted behind Autloc's back.

'To be wed.'

Barbara thought that taking a bride two days before one died willingly was absurd. 'To be wed and widowed in two days, what kind of marriage is that for an Aztec maiden?' she asked.

Tlotoxl's eyes glinted with secret pleasure. He had rehearsed Tonila well and Barbara had fallen into the trap.

Tonila argued that Aztec warriors frequently wed before going off to war and some did not return, but they were not proclaimed Gods as the Perfect Victim would be.

'There could be no greater honour,' he concluded.

'And if she wanted to marry again?'

Tonila shook his head vigorously. 'Marriage to a mortal would be unthinkable to the widow of a God.'

'So this maiden has defied your teachings and your law by spurning his proposal of marriage,' Barbara said, and when Tonila nodded, she thought 'Good for you, girl'. 'And what does the law prescribe for such an offence?' she asked.

Tonila waved his posy. 'We know of none. Such a rejection has never occurred before,' he replied, 'that is why we have sought your advice.'

Liar, Barbara thought and stared at Tlotoxl. 'She will not die,' her voice was adamant.

'Publicly ridiculed,' Tonila proposed.

Barbara thought that if there must be a punishment, ridicule would be relatively harmless.

Tlotoxl took a half-step forward. 'Scourged,' he hissed, 'her ears and tongue pierced with thorns.'

'I forbid it,' Barbara snapped.

'Autloc upholds it.' Tlotoxl's voice was a menace.

'Let him say so,' Barbara replied dryly.

'He will, he will,' Tonila assured her, 'when the time comes.'

'And when will that be?'

'On the day of darkness,' Tonila replied.

'Before all the people,' Tlotoxl made a sweeping gesture with his arm before pointing at Barbara, 'and you must be there so that the gravity of the offence is known.'

'I shall witness the punishment from the temple,' Barbara said, an idea formulating in her brain, 'but I wish my servants to be present with me. Ian, my aged servant, and my handmaiden.'

'It shall be arranged,' Tlotoxl said without expression, 'both the men and your handmaiden will be there. That I promise.'

As the High Priest of Sacrifice limped from the temple with Tonila at his side, Barbara sensed she had made a mistake somewhere. She went over their conversation several times in her head and then summoned the High Priest of Knowledge to the temple.

Autloc's face was grave as he listened to Barbara's account of her encounter with Tonila and the High Priest of Sacrifice.

'Tlotoxl insisted you upheld such bestial treatment. Is that true?' she asked.

'Is it still your intention to intervene at the sacrifice of the Perfect Victim?' Autloc countered.

'Of course, it is,' Barbara said firmly.

'Then I shall match your courage, Yetaxa,' he replied, 'though it grieves my heart, as it must yours.'

'I'll shed no tears over an end to human sacrifice.' Barbara was resolute.

'I was referring to your handmaiden,' Autloc explained.

'What about Susan?' Barbara asked sharply.

Autloc was perplexed. 'You have just spoken of her offence.'

Barbara jumped to her feet. 'Susan was to be the bride?' she exclaimed.

'Did not Tlotoxl say so?'

So that had been the trap, Barbara thought, a deliberate omission on Tlotoxl's part and a stupid one on hers.

'I shall forbid the punishment.'

'You cannot,' Autloc replied flatly.

'Oh yes, I can!' she said fiercely. 'Susan is to be punished at the eclipse so when you and I stop the human sacrifice then I will order Tlotoxl to release her as well.'

Autloc shook his head. 'She is to be punished before the sacrifice to the Sun God.'

'I won't let him harm her, I won't!' Barbara's voice

was final.

The High Priest looked at her. 'Will you, then, sacrifice all you believe in, all you have given me to believe, to save your handmaiden pain?'

Barbara had no answer.

11

Crawl, Swim, Climb

The moon was full and rode high in the star-studded sky as Ian slipped out of his quarters and crossed the courtyard silently and swiftly to the entrance. He wore only a warrior's loin-cloth and sandals, with a short stabbing sword slung on his hip. He opened the door, and sidled along the passageway which led to the main barracks. Ixta sneaked out of his quarters and followed him.

All was quiet as Ian hurried across the main courtyard to the gates at the far end. Ixta stayed in the shadow of the barrack-room walls while he stalked Ian, who went out onto the deserted streets and along the broad avenue which led to the pyramid and, behind it, the garden where the Doctor waited impatiently. Keeping his distance, Ixta followed.

Ian reached the door in the garden wall, but before he opened it he glanced up and down the avenue. Ixta ducked into the shadows of the pyramid and pressed himself against the side. Ian stepped into the garden and came face to face with the Doctor.

'I was beginning to worry about you, Chesterton,' he muttered.

'I waited until I knew the coast would be clear,' Ian murmured.

'So no one saw you,' the Doctor kept his voice down.

'No,' Ian replied softly.

'There's no one in the garden, either,' the Doctor hissed.

Then why are we whispering?' Ian asked out loud.

'Quite right, quite right,' the Doctor replied, and led Ian to the back wall, pulled aside the bougainvillea and showed him the carved snake on the stone. 'I've tried to move it, but it didn't budge an inch,' the Doctor said.

'Let me have a go.' Ian squatted down in front of the stone, unsheathed his stabbing sword and scraped the surrounds of the stone with the tip. 'Hardened clay,' he said. Some of the chippings came away, and he thrust the sword blade in deeper and deeper until it was up to the hilt. Then be began sawing away at the clay. As he did he felt the stone give. 'You're right, Doctor, look, the edges are bevelled so you can get a grip on them.' He showed the Doctor the slanted sides. 'But it'll take a few minutes to clear it.'

'We're not pressed for time, dear boy – not yet,' the Doctor replied.

Ixta watched the whole operation with great interest from behind a shrub.

When Ian had cleaned all the clay from around the stone, he could just manage to grip the bevelled sides with his fingertips. He put the sword back in its sheath and glanced up at the Doctor.

'Here goes,' he said, squeezing his fingertips against both sides he tried to pull the stone towards him.

To his surprise it slid out easily and he could soon put his hands underneath it. 'No wonder,' he remarked, 'it's greased,' and he lifted out the stone and laid it on the ground. He peered into the hole. 'It looks like a manhole to a tunnel, but I can't see very well.'

The Doctor took the pencil-torch from his breast pocket and handed it to Ian. 'Use that,' he said.

Ian shone the torch into the hole and explained that there was a six foot drop to the bottom of the tunnel which seemed to be about three feet high but handholds had been gouged in the stones so that one could get back up.

Ixta had been on the point of challenging them, but the torch had frightened him, so he remained concealed.

'You stay guard, Chesterton,' the Doctor said as Ian wriggled backwards out of the hole.

'No, Doctor, you stay guard, I'll go in.'

'Then both of us will go,' the Doctor insisted.

Ian grinned. 'You're hardly dressed for a spelaeological crawl,' he observed as he handed the torch to the Doctor.

Instinctively, Ixta cowered back behind the bushes, wondering what magic Ian possessed to be able to make light without fire.

Ian turned around and slid, feet first, into the hole. Reaching the bottom of the tunnel would mean about a two-foot drop once he released the outside of the hole, as the greased lining would not allow him to hold on.

'If all goes well, Doctor,' he said cheerfully, 'I'll meet you at the garden gate again.'

'Good luck, Chesterton,' the Doctor replied as Ian let go and dropped from sight.

As he hit the bottom of the tunnel his feet shot out from underneath him and he grabbed the handholds to keep his balance.

'Here's the torch. Catch,' the Doctor called and threw it into the hole.

Ian grabbed it and shone the light first in one direction and then in the other. The base and sides of the tunnel were square but the top was vaulted. One way was about ten feet long and ended at what appeared to be a wall. In the other direction the tunnel stretched beyond the range of the torch towards the temple. Ian crouched to enter the tunnel but the bottom was too slippery so he got down on all fours realising that, joking aside, he really was in for a time-consuming spelaeological crawl.

With the lit torch clamped between his teeth and protruding from his mouth, Ian made his way along the tunnel.

The Doctor watched as the light reflected off the walls faded, until it disappeared altogether. Having regained his courage now that Ian's magic light had gone, Ixta watched the Doctor as he bent down to examine the stone. He tried to lift it but it was too heavy. Then he noticed the two handles hewn in the back and realised that it could be slid into place from the inside, convincing him that he had not sent Ian off on a wild goose chase.

Silently Ixta crept away towards the garden door which he opened and slammed shut. The Doctor heard the noise and re-arranged the bougainvillea, but part of the stone remained visible. Then he sauntered away along the path. Ixta selected one that would enable him to intercept the Doctor. He wandered along it, admiring the night sky. When he met the Doctor he smiled. 'I greet the aged servant of Yetaxa.' He bowed. 'It is a pleasant night to walk abroad.'

'Yes, I couldn't sleep so I thought a stroll in the garden would be agreeable,' the Doctor replied.

'We are well met,' Ixta said, 'for I would talk to you about Ian, with whom I must soon dispute the command of our armies.' He walked down the path the Doctor had come along, making sure that he was on the wall side.

'Oh, yes?' the Doctor was obliged to turn back.

'I do not believe I can defeat him,' Ixta admitted, 'for, as the servant of Yetaxa, he has powers of which I know nothing.'

'True,' the Doctor concurred, glancing at the partially visible stone out of the corner of his eye.

'Thus we are unfairly matched in any contest,' Ixta stated.

'Inevitably, I suppose.'

'Then what am I to do? Of all Aztec warriors I am the most fit to command,' he edged his way towards the stone, 'I have proved myself again and again, but I am no match for the servant of a God.'

The Doctor took Ixta by the arm and tried to steer him away from the stone. 'What you say is true.' The Doctor tugged at him gently. 'And I shall ask Yetaxa to demand that Ian renounces his role as a Chosen Warrior.'

'Would you do that for me?' Ixta exclaimed and, breaking away from the Doctor's grip, stepped backwards onto the stone. 'Ouch!' he cried.

'What's the matter?' The Doctor tried to look startled.

Ixta swept the bougainvillea aside revealing both the stone and the hole. 'What negligence is this?' he demanded. 'The stone must be replaced.'

'I'm sure whoever took it out did so for a very good reason,' the Doctor said and suggested they left it where it was.

'But this part of the garden will be ruined,' Ixta protested.

'Why should that be?' the Doctor asked.

'There is a tunnel which is used to irrigate the garden. My father's father built it.'

'I am aware of that,' the Doctor remarked dryly.

'This entrance was made so that the tunnel could be

inspected and cleaned from time to time,' Ixta explained, 'but if the stone is not put back the next time the sluice-gate is opened the water will pour out and flood this area. No, it must be replaced.' Ixta picked it up, slid it back into the wall and then tapped all around the edges with the heel of his fist to ensure that the stone was firmly in. He stood up and smiled at the Doctor. 'Pardon my insistence, but I am proud of all that my father's father did.'

'With good reason,' the Doctor replied.

'You will speak on my behalf to Yetaxa?' the Chosen Warrior asked.

'Of course, of course, I have given my word,' the Doctor sounded sardonic.

'Then I shall bid you a peaceful night,' Ixta said, bowed, and strode away towards the garden door.

The Doctor watched and waited until Ixta had gone outside, then he tried to prise out the stone but he didn't have the strength. If I am wrong and it is only a tunnel, at least Ian can push the stone out from the inside, he thought, but Ixta's sudden appearance troubled him nonetheless.

As soon as he was outside the garden, Ixta did not walk towards the pyramid but went in the opposite direction. He came to the back wall which he followed until he reached the reservoir and the sluice-gate. He chuckled as he released it, letting the water cascade into the tunnel.

'Now use your magic to save yourself, Ian,' he said and walked away.

The sound the Doctor heard was a whispered gurgling, but he knew exactly what it was. 'Chesterton!' he cried out in horror, and ran towards the garden door, knowing full well that it was a futile gesture as no one would have the strength to close the sluice-gate against the water pressure until the reservoir was almost empty.

Ian still could not see the end of the tunnel when he had the first indication of trouble. It was a breeze coming from behind him which built quickly into a gust of wind and then he heard the water hissing and gurgling as it rushed towards him. Suddenly the water hit him and threw him of balance. 'Go with it,' he shouted to himself, 'while there's air,' and straightening out he began swimming desperately with the building wall of water.

It had reached the height of the sides and had begun to fill the vaulted top before Ian saw the wall at the end. It was solid. Lifting his head he shone the torch on the top looking for a trapdoor or a vertical shaft that would give him a chance to escape. There was none. The water level was about two inches from the highest point of the vault and still rising when Ian touched the wall. He took the torch from his mouth, put his head back and gulped in two deep breaths of air, the last, he believed, of his life. He put his feet down to touch the bottom of the tunnel and found that he could stand upright. Though the tunnel was full, water still swirled past his feet. Completely underwater he reached down and touched the opening of a second lower tunnel. If I'm to die, I'll die finding out, Ian thought and crouched down to force himself into it.

He clawed his way along. His lungs were bursting as he reached the end and shot up to the surface in a small chamber with plenty of airspace. Just beneath the surface of the water there was a ledge against one wall. Ian grabbed hold of it, gasping for air, then hauled himself up onto it. He shone the light onto the water: it had stopped rising. He played the torch on the ceiling and saw a three-foot square shaft directly above his head. On two opposing walls were nine-inch oblong stones projecting into the shaft and staggered at three-foot intervals. Ian estimated that there must be eighty of them to climb to reach the temple. He decided to give himself a few moments more to catch his breath and shone the torch along the ledge. In one corner was a white circular object. Ian reached out and picked it up. It was a human skull. With a shudder he put it back on the ledge and shone the light onto the water in the chamber. On the bottom he could see bits and pieces of a disintegrated human skeleton. I know who you are, Ian thought, Ixta's father and it wouldn't surprise me in the least if your son had tried to drown me by opening the sluice-gate. But what happened to you?, Ian wondered as he stood up. Putting the torch back between his teeth, he placed one foot on the first stone in the wall and reached up to haul himself into the shaft. Straddling the sides, Ian began to climb, testing each stone before using it, first as a handhold and subsequently as a foothold. At the same time he mentally ticked them off.

It was slow, arduous work and he had counted to fifty-seven when he saw the reason for Ixta's father's death. A stone had broken away from the wall. Ian paused. So far during the climb his weight had always been taken on two stones and most of the time on three. With a stone missing there was a twelve-foot gap between the foothold and the next handhold on one side. To negotiate it meant that there would be a moment when all his weight rested on one stone on the opposite side and if it snapped, he would join Ixta's father one hundred and seventy feet below. It was too dangerous, so he backed down until he had a handhold and a double foothold, then he lifted one leg off its stone perch and put it against the wall in front of him. At the same time he leaned his back against the wall behind him and stiffened his leg to wedge himself between the two sides. Then he released his handhold and placed his palms on either side of his back. Gingerly he brought his other leg up to the front wall. Maintaining the pressure against both sides with his legs, back and hands, he inched his way up the shaft, past the broken stone until he could safely resume two footholds and a handhold again. Only then did it occur to him that when Ixta's father fell, the stones must have torn him to shreds. Ian swallowed and started on up again.

Sixty, sixty-one, sixty-two ... until seventy-eight, when the torch lit another small chamber. Ian hauled himself into it. He took the torch from his mouth and looked around. Against one wall were some proper steps which led to the ceiling. Ian mounted them, put his hands on the stone immediately above his head, pushed it up and slid it to one side. He took the two remaining stairs in a stride, and shone the torch on Yetaxa's skeleton on the slab. Then he turned to the TARDIS and smiled.

'Mid temples and barrackses though we may roam,' he sang quietly, 'be it ever so humble, there's no place like home.' And he went inside.

12

Wall of Deception

Barbara was in the antechamber trying to sleep, but every time she closed her eyes she had nightmarish visions of Susan's punishment, Ian's death in a fight with Ixta, her own public denouncement as a false God, with

Tlotoxl cutting out her heart, and the Doctor driven insane meandering in the garden babbling inanities to himself. With her eyes open, there wasn't much of an improvement. Both the Doctor and Ian had impressed upon her the importance of her role as Yetaxa, but the tension of playing the part was bringing her close to breaking-point. She needed to do something, not just be something, to help them out of their plight. She sat up on the couch, put her elbows on her knees and held her head in her hands.

'Come on, Barbara Wright,' she said aloud, 'you must not crack.' She stood up and clutched her arms across her chest. Then she heard the Doctor arguing with the temple guard outside.

'But I must speak to Yetaxa,' the Doctor snapped.

'It is forbidden.' The guard was adamant.

'A damnation on being forbidden,' the Doctor exploded. 'Out of my way.'

Quickly Barbara opened the door. 'Let my aged servant pass,' she commanded.

In obedience the guard stood to one side, but said that the Doctor's presence would be reported.

'So be it,' Barbara slammed the door in the guard's face. Then she looked at the Doctor. His face was ashen.

'Doctor, those stairs . . .' she began.

The Doctor shook his head. 'It's young Chesterton,' he said.

'What about Ian?' Barbara asked in alarm.

'I think he's dead,' the Doctor replied in remorse, 'drowned by Ixta. And it was all my fault.'

For a moment Barbara was stunned, incapable of grasping the enormity of the Doctor's statement. Then, as it sunk in, one word came through to the forefront of her mind. 'You said "think", Doctor. Does that mean you don't know, that you are not sure?' she asked, clutching at a straw.

The Doctor told her everything that had happened in the garden.

'Then there's still hope,' Barbara said, taking the Doctor's hand, 'but this is not the place to be,' she added and led him up to the temple.

Inside the TARDIS Ian looked for some cord, string, even a length of flex would do, but no, there were only printed circuits. Enough of sophisticated electronics that keep going wrong, he thought. Wherever we land next, let's get back to Boy Scout basics: a length of string and a knife with a thing for taking stones out of horses' hooves. He went out into the tomb and shone the torch around. Under Yetaxa's skeleton was a cotton sheet with a narrow silk border sewn onto it. Ian found the join, unpicked it and then carefully ripped the silk away from the cotton which had rotted over the decades. He carried the strip of silk over to the fresco and looked for a place to attach it. The eagle's neck stood proud from the wall, like the eye of a needle, so Ian threaded one end of the silk through it and tied a knot. He tugged the silk several times to make sure it would hold. Then he pushed outwards on the wall and stepped into the temple.

'Chesterton, my dear chap, you're alive,' the Doctor exclaimed and embraced him. 'I was afraid you were drowned.'

'I very nearly was,' Ian replied and began to recount his adventure in the tunnel.

Suddenly, Barbara interrupted him. 'The wall's closing,' she cried in alarm.

Ian held up the end of the strip of silk.

'It doesn't matter,' he said, 'the other end is attached to the fresco on the inside and, as the wall is counterbalanced, all we need to do is tug on this end and we're home and away.'

The Doctor thought this was an over-simplification but he said nothing as he still felt guilty about the tunnel.

'Why don't you two go through to the TARDIS whilst I go to the seminary and fetch Susan?' Ian suggested.

'No.' The Doctor was firm. 'When we go to the other side of that wall we all go together. Splitting up is not a good idea.'

Barbara agreed and added that fetching Susan might not be as simple a task as Ian imagined.

'Why not?' Ian asked.

Barbara explained about Susan's refusal to marry the Perfect Victim and described her punishment for denying his wish. 'Knowing Tlotoxl, she's bound to be guarded,' Barbara concluded.

'And knowing Ixta, she won't be in the seminary,' Ian added, 'he'll keep her a prisoner in his quarters. So, wait for us in the antechamber, it's more comfortable than up here.' He winked at them and started towards the brocade curtain.

'Watch out for Ixta, Chesterton,' the Doctor felt obliged to warn him, 'he's a wily devil.'

Ian stopped aned grinned.

'But I'll have the psychological advantage, Doctor. He thinks I'm dead,' he replied and hurried away.

Barbara and the Doctor hid the silk strip behind the curtain in praise of Tloloc, the God of Water, which still covered the entrance to the tomb.

Barbara and Ian were right on all counts. Tlotoxl had two guards accompany him and Susan from the seminary to the barracks and Ixta's quarters, where he told the warriors to remain outside with Susan until he commanded them to enter. He went inside and Ixta, after paying his respects, told the High Priest of the events in the garden. Tlotoxl congratulated him on his success and added that, with Ian dead, the others were at their mercy.

'The rewards I promised you shall be yours,' Tlotoxl said, 'and when the Perfect Victim is sacrificed to Huitzilipochtli and the sun's light shines again on our land, then I shall proclaim you commander of our armies.'

'I shall serve the High Priest well,' Ixta assured him.

'Let your service begin now,' Tlotoxl said and ordered the warriors to bring in Susan. 'I leave her in your charge, Ixta,' he continued, 'do not let her escape nor release her to Autloc, whose faith in Huitzilipochtli falters.'

Susan demanded to know why she had been taken from the seminary, but Tlotoxl was evasive and would only say that it was for her safekeeping.

'Does Yetaxa know that I am here?' Susan insisted.

'A true God is all-knowing, all-seeing,' he sneered.

'As the Great Spirit's handmaiden, I demand to be escorted to the temple and shown into her presence,' she persisted.

'And so you shall, at the appointed time.'

Susan shivered involuntarily at the cold menace in his voice.

He turned back to Ixta. 'Guard her,' he ordered, and limped out of the quarters with the two warriors.

Ixta pointed to the bedroom. 'You may rest in there.'

'I'm not tired,' Susan said and sat on a cushion.

Ixta shrugged. 'Nor am I, nor shall I be, whilst I am charged with you,' he warned, facing her with his back to the entrance.

Ian had just enough time to tuck into the shadows of the main barracks when he saw Tlotoxl and the warriors coming through the passageway from the courtyard. He waited until they had gone past before he slipped into it and stealthily made his way, back pressed against the wall, towards Ixta's quarters.

'Do you know where Ian is?' the Chosen Warrior was asking Susan.

'You'd be surprised, Ian thought, but he didn't catch Susan's reply.

'Then I shall tell you. He's dead,' Ixta announced.

'I don't believe you,' Ian heard Susan shout.

'The old man was there when he died,' Ixta continued, 'he knows it to be true. Now have seven warriors, one of whom was the servant of a God, challenged my right to command,' his voice rang with pride, 'and I alone survive.'

'Not true,' Ian said as he stepped up behind Ixta and hit him with a cross-handed, double-razor chop on either side of his neck which made the Chosen Warrior's eyes almost pop out of his head before he collapsed unconscious on the floor. 'Good commanders never jump to conclusions,' Ian added with a grin.

'Ian,' Susan gasped, 'I knew he was lying. He tried to make me believe you were dead.'

Ian put his arm around her. 'He was a couple of seconds short of the truth,' Ian replied and then asked if she had her everyday clothes with her. Susan pointed to a bundle on the floor.

'They made me bring everything from the seminary.'

'How terribly obliging of them.' Ian picked up the bundle and led her across the courtyard to his quarters, where he gathered up his ordinary clothes.

'Where are we going?' Susan asked.

'To the TARDIS. Where else?' he answered.

As they left Ian enquired how Susan had found her school. She pulled a face. 'Not much better than yours in England.'

Dawn streaked the sky as Barbara waited anxiously in the antechamber with the Doctor, who was scribbling mathematical formulae on a pocket notepad.

'I hope they're all right,' Barbara said.

'I've come to the conclusion that young Chesterton is a remarkably resourceful chap,' the Doctor remarked, grimacing as he rechecked his calculations.

'I just want us to get away as quickly as possible,' Barbara confessed.

The Doctor looked up at her. 'And history?' he asked.

'Can remain unchanged,' she replied.

'No rewriting?'

'None.'

The Doctor nodded and tapped the notepad with his pencil.

'It won't be easy, you know, my dear.'

Barbara looked puzzled. 'What won't?' she asked.

'Opening up the wall. I've been doing some calculations and I don't believe we have the strength,' he replied.

'Doctor, I barely touched the wall and it began to swing open.'

'From the inside, Barbara,' the Doctor reminded her, and explained that the pressure of her hand on the inside of the wall was both a force outwards and upwards because of the counterbalance but now with the strip of silk attached to the fresco, the first force was downwards to the foot of the wall and the second one was outwards.

'But where is the upwards thrust?' he asked her.

'The counterbalance swinging down will supply it,' Barbara replied.

The Doctor shook his head. 'No, my dear, things don't tend to move unless ...'

'... you start the ball rolling,' Barbara finished for him.

'Precisely,' the Doctor said, 'and downwards and outwards is not the same thing as outwards and upwards. What's more,' he added, 'that bit of silk is almost a hundred years old and it won't take too much strain.'

'What can we do?' Barbara asked.

'Try,' the Doctor replied, as he slipped the notepad back into his pocket.

At that moment Susan and Ian came breathlessly into the antechamber. 'Anyone for the *Skylark*?' Ian gasped.

Barbara and the Doctor exchanged a quick apprehensive glance and the four of them went up to the temple. Barbara took the silk from behind the curtain as the Doctor looked at Ian.

'I'm sorry, my dear fellow, but this may not work,' the Doctor said apologetically, 'and we can't put too much load on the silk because it will break.'

They began tugging on the silk, but nothing happened.

'What if I push in at the top of the wall while you pull out at the bottom?' Ian suggested.

'It's from the inside out, Chesterton, not from the outside in,' the Doctor said, 'you're up against the law of . . .'

'Inertia!' Ian exploded. 'Of all the stupid things to overlook. I only had to put it around the doorknob of the TARDIS or something and it would have pulled the counterbalance in.'

None of the others said a word.

'All right.' Ian looked at each of them in turn. 'I'll do the tunnel and the climb again and open the wall from the inside.'

'The stone has handgrips on the back. Fit it in the wall again, just in case,' the Doctor cautioned and gave him the pencil-torch. 'And, Chesterton, a final warning – Ixta.'

Ian grinned and looked at Susan. 'When last seen the Chosen Warrior had deserted Huitzilipochtli for a Greek God whose name is Morpheus. Right, Susan?'

13

False God

Ixta groaned, struggled to his feet, stumbled into the bathroom and splashed water onto his throbbing head. Then holding the sides of his neck, he tried to remember what had happened. At first, all he could recall was the blinding flash of light inside his head and a sensation of falling. His befuddled wits told him he had been hit from behind, but he had not seen nor heard anyone approaching. Why not, he wondered and dragged out the answer from the grey cloud inside his skull. He had had his back to the entrance. The next piece of information he wanted was why he would have been like that. His aching brain told him he had been talking. To whom? And as if someone had thrown a bucket of ice cold water over him, he remembered. He staggered back into the main room. No one was there, nor was the bundle. He checked the bedroom, but it was empty. He reeled across the courtyard and went into Ian's quarters. There was no sign of life but, reluctantly, Ixta's intelligence had to concede that Ian was still alive and that it had been Ian who struck him down. He picked up the cudgel that had been assigned to Ian and went out into the early morning light with two enterprises in mind: to recover Susan for Tlotoxl, and kill Ian for himself.

Ixta met the High Priest of Sacrifice in front of the pyramid and Tlotoxl listened angrily while the shamefaced Chosen Warrior made his report.

'But I shall recapture the handmaiden,' he promised, and brandishing the cudgel, he swore to kill Ian with his own club.

Tlotoxl's eyes narrowed. 'That belongs to Ian?' he asked.

'I took it from his quarters,' Ixta replied.

'Let him live a little longer,' the High Priest said and tapped the cudgel with his forefinger. 'I have a better purpose for that. Every day at this time Autloc meditates in the garden of peace. Go and strike him down from behind but not to kill.'

Ixta was horrified. 'Strike down the High Priest,' he exclaimed, 'there is no greater offence.'

Tlotoxl ignored the protest and told Ixta to throw the cudgel into the bushes nearby where it would be found and identified. 'That will destroy Autloc's faith in Yetaxa's divinity and tomorow when the darkness comes, she and her servants will be opposed by all who worship Huitzilipochtli. Now, do as I bid you,' he ordered and Ixta, under the High Priest's mesmeric gaze, nodded and strode off towards the garden.

Tlotoxl went into the pyramid and began to climb the stairs, but drew into the shadows when he heard footsteps hurrying down. Ian passed him, taking the stairs two at a time. Tlotoxl followed and saw that Ian, too, was making for the garden.

'This time, Ixta, do not fail me,' he murmured and went in search of the temple guards.

Ixta's mission was easily accomplished. Autloc was sitting by himself on a bench looking at the lake, so the Chosen Warrior slunk up behind and rapped him smartly on the back of the head, making sure that no obsidian stone penetrated his skull. Autloc slumped to the ground and Ixta threw the cudgel into some bushes close by. He heard the garden door open, ducked down and watched as Ian made his way to the back wall and the entrance to the tunnel. Then Tlotoxl and four temple guards came into the garden. Keeping his head down, Ixta ran over to them, nodded slightly to the High Priest and pointed at Ian who was pulling aside the bougainvillea in front of the stone.

'Seize him,' Tlotoxl hissed.

The guards raced over to Ian who was now crouched in front of the stone getting a grip on the sides with his fingertips. He looked up and saw four javelins pointing at him and decided that it was not a moment to dispute the toss. He rose slowly to his feet as Tlotoxl, flourishing the cudgel, and Ixta, supporting Autloc, came along the path.

'Take him to the barracks and imprison him,' Tlotoxl ordered, 'for he struck down the High Priest of Knowledge.'

'That's not true, Autloc,' Ian said.

'This is your club,' Tlotoxl replied. 'Ixta, the Chosen Warrior, has identified it.' And left his fingerprints all over it, Ian thought as he was led away, while Autloc, much to Tlotoxl's delight, cried out that he had served a false God.

Barbara, Susan and the Doctor were anxiously awaiting Ian's appearance when Tonila, three women with a large folded curtain, and two guards carrying a ladder came into the temple. Tonila looked curiously at Susan but said nothing. He clapped his hands and the guards propped up the ladder beside the corner of the back wall. One of them went to the top and unlaced one end of the curtain in honour of Tlaloc, the God of Water, which fell to the ground. Barbara, Susan and the Doctor looked at one another in alarm as the guards moved the ladder to the other end of the wall. One of them climbed up and started to unlace the other side of the curtain. Barbara glanced quickly at Tonila, the women, and the guard at the foot of the ladder. All eyes were on the one unlacing the curtain. She turned to Susan.

'In respect for the God Tlaloc, break the fall of the curtain,' she commanded.

Susan bowed, ran to the corner, put her foot behind the curtain and swept the coiled strip of silk under her monastic robe as the curtain fell into her arms. The Doctor twiddled his thumbs in relief. The women came over with a corner of the new curtain which was handed up to be laced. The rest was laid out along the foot of the wall and the old curtain scooped up. Susan didn't move, keeping her foot firmly clamped on the strip of silk under her robe. The ladder was moved back to its original position and the other end of the curtain laced into place. Susan discretely pushed back the strip of silk behind it. The new curtain was blood red with the head of Huitzilipochtli woven with gold thread in the centre. Rays of sunlight radiated from it, but the face was sinister, the eyes cruel and the mouth hard. Barbara lookd at it and knew that the sooner they were quit of the Aztecs the better.

As soon as Tonila, the women and the guards had left the temple, the Doctor congratulated Barbara for her quick thinking and Susan for her fast reaction.

'I was concerned that Ian would open the wall while they were changing the curtain,' Susan admitted.

'If I could have one wish granted,' Barbara replied, 'it's that he should open it now.'

But nothing happened until Tonila returned with four

temple guards, Ixta, and Tlotoxl, who sidled over to Barbara.

'Your servant, Ian, is to die for striking down the High Priest of Knowledge and your handmaiden will be doubly punished for attempting to escape the scourging and piercing with thorns. Now her eyes will be put out.' Tlotoxl relished the moment when Susan screamed as Ixta took her by the arm. She struggled to free herself hitting him repeatedly with her fist.

'Stop that, Susan,' the Doctor was brusque, but his voice softened as he told her to go quietly with Ixta.

Barbara looked with loathing at Tlotoxl. 'You will kill my servant and you will blind and torture my handmaiden?' She pointed to the Doctor. 'What fate have you in store for my aged servant?'

Tlotoxl spread out his arms. 'None. The old man has not transgressed our laws.' The insinuation was evident. 'Let him sit in peace in the garden,' and Tlotoxl ordered the guards to escort him there. The Doctor looked at Barbara and momentarily clenched his fists to tell her to hold on. Barbara understood and when there were only Tonila, Tlotoxl and herself, she mounted the dais and sat on the throne.

'And me, Tlotoxl?' she asked. The High Priest of Sacrifice had vengeance in his eyes as he pointed to the curtain behind her.

'You tried to deny Huitzilipochtli his right to human blood. You tried to humiliate us with a false faith. And by your own admission you are not a God. I have always known it. The Priest of Knowledge, Tonila, knows it and now the High Priest, Autloc, knows it,' Tlotoxl crowed. 'Sit there until Huitzilipochtli accepts our perfect sacrifice and as he gives light back to the earth your entrails will tell the Aztec nation of your deception.' He turned his back on her and with Tonila waddling at his side, he limped away from the temple.

A few minutes ago, Barbara thought, I believed we were within an ace of being free. Now, our plight is worse than it ever was and all I can do is hang on, as the Doctor asked me to.

As soon as he was released by the guards, the Doctor went to the garden shed, found the stump of a dead bush, sawed off a section and, sitting himself down on a bench outside, he began to whittle away at it. He was working quietly when Cameca saw him.

'Of all the Aztecs, the High Priest of Knowledge is the most gentle,' she said reproachfully.

The Doctor concentrated on his piece of wood. 'Ian didn't hit him, my dear,' he replied.

'His club was found nearby,' she countered.

'Planted nearby.' The Doctor peeled off a sliver of wood.

'He is to die.' Cameca sat down beside the Doctor.

'No doubt. Butchered by Ixta.' The Doctor blew off some shavings.

Cameca reached out and placed her hand gently on his knee. 'If it is your wish,' she said, 'let our marriage be postponed.'

The Doctor looked at her in silence for a moment and then began to carve a groove around the rim of the piece of wood.

'What is that you make?' Cameca asked softly.

'Something to take my mind off my problems.'

'Will you permit me to intercede with the High Priest of Knowledge on your friend's behalf?'

The Doctor placed the piece of wood with the knife on the bench and took her hand between both of his. 'If you will, I should be eternally grateful to you,' the Doctor said, 'but it is Tlotoxl we must contend with.' He gestured to the garden. 'All this, the peace you know, will one day be destroyed by him and others like him.'

'If it is the will of the Gods, it cannot be prevented.'

'It was not Quetzecoatl's will, nor is it Yetaxa's,' the Doctor replied.

'You say the Gods wish an end to sacrifice.' Cameca sought to understand.

'Yetaxa speaks for them, but without Autloc's faith in her their words are wasted,' he explained.

Cameca stood up. 'His faith shall be restored, I promise you, beloved,' and she hurried away.

The Doctor stared after her. In another world, in another time, he mused, then picked up the wood and the knife to get on with the job in hand.

The High Priest of Knowledge stood rigid in front of the throne. Barbara smiled and thanked him for attending her.

'Such gratitude is due to Cameca,' Autloc replied formally.

'Then say it to her for me,' Barbara said and Autloc bowed. 'Ian did not strike you down.' The High Priest looked at her directly.

'The evidence, Great Spirit, would indicate that he did,' Autloc replied, 'the club was his and he was in the garden of peace.'

'As were, by a strange coincidence, Tlotoxl, Ixta and four temple guards,' Barbara added.

Autloc conceded that the High Priest of Sacrifice sought to destroy Yetaxa as a false God.

'He has every intention of doing so,' Barbara said. 'Indeed, he has given me a graphic description of the manner in which I shall die. He has also announced that my handmaiden, Susan, will have her eyes gouged out' – Autloc winced – 'for daring to escape with Ian, who is now condemned for a crime he did not commit. In fact, the only detail the High Priest of Sacrifice has left unsaid is the manner of Ian's death.'

Autloc looked uncomfortably at his posy. 'Ixta will throw him from the parapet just before the darkness comes,' he murmured.

Barbara stood and came down from the throne. She circled the High Priest. 'What manner of people are you?' she demanded in indignation, 'who wallow in virtue and in bestiality? You Aztecs are schizophrenics.'

Autloc looked at her uncomprehendingly for a moment, then the realisation dawned in his eyes. 'You Aztecs,' he repeated. 'What manner of people are you? Yes, I yield ground to Tlotoxl on one point. You are not the Great Spirit of Yetaxa. You are not of our nation. I know not who you are nor from whence you and your servants come.' He pointed to the blood-red curtain. 'That secret is sealed in Yetaxa's tomb. A God you may be, but none of my knowing.' He walked away from Barbara, his posy of flowers against his chin, then turned to face her again. 'You have prophesied our annihilation if human sacrifice continues, yet you have always spoken softly with respect and affection.'

'There is a legend I have heard, told to me by a wanderer from the desert, of another God far across the oceans, who spoke as you have spoken of gentleness and love, who was taken by those who opposed him and crucified as we crucify common thieves.'

Barbara did not reply.

Autloc looked away, and then turned back to her. 'What I can do, I shall do,' he said. 'Farewell.' And he walked with dignity from the temple.

14

Day of Darkness

It was almost finished. The groove encircled the rim and the Doctor had bored a round hole through the centre of the wood, both sides of which he bevelled on the corner of the stone bench. He put his forefinger through the hole to check the smoothness and then spun it with the other hand. It rotated freely and was well balanced. He took it off his finger and looked at it with a certain pride. He had never made a pulley-wheel before.

He became aware of being watched and looked up. Cameca was standing a few yards away. He stood up and she came over to him.

'I have spoken to Autloc and he went to see Yetaxa,' she said.

'Thank you, my dear,' the Doctor replied.

Cameca looked at the pulley-wheel. 'It is finished?' she asked.

'Almost.'

'As is our time together, beloved.' Tentatively she touched the pulley-wheel. 'I do not understand its purpose but I have always known that it would take you away from me.'

The Doctor put it in his pocket and took her hands in his. 'I am very sorry, my dear,' was all he could say.

'Tomorrow will truly be a day of darkness,' Cameca said sadly.

'For both of us,' the Doctor replied.

Cameca gripped his hands. 'Why is Tlotoxl so determined to destroy Yetaxa?' Her voice was fierce.

'To safeguard his own beliefs,' the Doctor said.

Cameca released his hands and bowed her head. 'We are a doomed people,' she whispered, 'and there is no turning back for us.'

A lump came to the Doctor's throat and he had to swallow hard before he could reply. 'You are a fine woman, Cameca, and you will always be very, very, dear to me.'

Autloc discretely cleared his throat as he approached them. 'I have spoken to whomever the deity is who wears the coiled serpent of Yetaxa on her arm,' he said with a half-smile.

The Doctor put his hand to his pocket, felt the outline of the pulley-wheel, and thought, that's it.

'And I promised to do all that I could to help her handmaiden and her young warrior.'

'Thank you,' the Doctor replied respectfully.

Autloc turned to Cameca. 'I would speak with you alone, Cameca,' he said.

She glanced at the Doctor who smiled and nodded.

Autloc looked back at him. 'Farewell,' he said. 'I shall pray to Quetzecoatl that you may all re-enter the tomb of Yetaxa in safety.'

'May your prayers be heard,' the Doctor replied and he watched them walk away.

Tears glistened in Cameca's eyes.

'You are sad,' Autloc observed.

'I have lost all that is dear to my heart,' she replied.

'These visitors have touched the essence of our being,' Autloc said, 'and to ignore it would be to deny that which I was, the High Priest of Knowledge.'

Cameca looked at him sharply. 'You are no longer?' she asked.

He shook his head. 'I have lost faith in Huitzilipochtli and in our traditions.'

'Then your tragedy is far greater than mine,' Cameca said. 'Your entire life has been devoted to the temple. Mine has encompassed but a few days.' They walked along the path leading to the garden door.

'We have known each other in trust for many years and I have sought your counsel frequently, Cameca,' he admitted. 'Perhaps in another nation you would have been the High Priest of Knowledge and I, a seller of vegetables.'

She smiled at the concept.

'Now, I wish you to do something for me to assist them,' he continued and took a gold medallion and chain from around his neck, 'this is the title to my dwelling-place and all I own therein.' He put it in her hand. 'Tomorrow whilst Ixta prepares the Perfect Victim for sacrifice, the handmaiden and the warrior, Ian, will be brought together under guard before they are escorted to the temple for their punishment.' He squeezed the medallion in her hand. 'Give that to the guard so that he turns his head away while you conduct the girl, as if for punishment, to the temple.'

'And Ian, the warrior?' Cameca asked.

Autloc smiled. 'I am sure he will accompany you,' he said.

'I shall do it,' Cameca replied, and then asked Autloc about himself.

'You have nothing. What will you do? Where will you go?'

'Into the wilderness, Cameca,' he said, 'to seek the truth of Quetzecoatl.'

'When?'

'Now,' he replied. 'What better time?' He laid his posy of flowers on a bench and walked out of the garden.

Cameca thought to return to the Doctor and tell him about the medallion but decided that had that been Autloc's wish, he would have spoken to her in the Doctor's presence. So she picked up Autloc's posy as a memento and went home.

With the dawn came tension as the Aztecs watched the sun begin the journey across the clear blue sky to its zenith, when all knew day would become night. In their minds was one question, would Huitzilipochli accept the sacrifice of the Perfect Victim and give them back his light, which was their life, or would they be left to die in eternal darkness? Families stayed in their homes until the appointed hour when they would be summoned to the temple square to pay reverence to the Perfect Victim and, in fear and trembling, worship their Sun God.

The door of Ian's dark, cramped barracks cell was opened by an armed warrior and the daylight flooded in. Ian blinked several times then went outside where a second warrior pointed with his cudgel towards the Chosen Warrior's courtyard. Ian walked through the passageway and wondered if this would be his final encounter with Ixta, if he would have a small red circle painted over his heart and have a javelin hurled at it as though he were a life-size clay model. To his surprise he was directed to his old quarters where two warriors stood at either side of the entrance. He went inside and Susan, guarded by another warrior, threw herself into his arms.

'What's to happen to us, Ian?' she asked in desperation.

'We're to be taken to the temple,' Ian replied, 'and you know what that means, don't you?'

'Horrible things!' She sounded terrified.

'No, the four of us will be together again,' Ian said reassuringly, 'and thinking about it overnight I've come to the conclusion that Tlotoxl and his friends are no match for the Doctor.'

Across the courtyard in Ixta's quarters the Perfect Victim waited in impatient, drugged euphoria for his deification. His body had been washed and perfumed, his garments were radiantly white, his plumed helmet extravagantly colourful and in his hands he held an exotic posy of flowers and a fly-swatter.

Ixta came from his bedroom wearing the Chosen Warrior's full ceremonial dress. 'It will be my privilege as leader of our armies to escort you, O Perfect Victim, to your glory,' he intoned.

The Perfect Victim smiled. 'May victory always sit upon your shoulders,' he replied.

Tonila waddled in. 'Let the procession begin,' he said. 'The avenues are lined.'

Ixta looked at Tonila sharply. 'And what of the girl and my challenger?' he asked.

'They will follow at a distance and by another way so that the Perfect Victim's path to the temple is not defiled before the sacrifice,' Tonila replied.

'They should go first,' Ixta argued.

'The High Priest of Sacrifice does not wish it,' Tonila said. 'They follow the Perfect Victim, but will be punished first. I shall instruct the guard,' he added and made his way across the courtyard to give explicit instructions to the warrior accompanying Susan and Ian about the route he should take to the temple. Then Tonila hurried away so as not to miss his moment of reflected glory.

The Aztecs watched in awed silence as the Perfect Victim walked slowly along the broad, warrior-lined avenue towards the pyramid and the temple. On one side of him was Tonila, supposedly gazing intently at his posy but his eyes flicked from side to side at the crowd as he tried to gauge the impression he was making. On the other side of the Perfect Victim was Ixta, proudly carrying a gold-studded cudgel, the insignia of the commander of the Aztec armies. But despite the solemnity of the moment, every few seconds someone in the crowd would shield their eyes and look up apprehensively at the sun blazing down on them.

Cameca hurried across the deserted barracks courtyard and went through the passageway. The two warriors outside Ian's quarters saluted her as she passed them as did the third one inside.

'What brings you here, Cameca?' he asked.

'I have been instructed by the High Priests to escort Yetaxa's handmaiden to the temple,' she answered.

The warrior glanced at Ian.'What of him?'

'You, alone, will escort him. So dismiss the others,' she replied.

'I cannot do that,' the warrior said warily. 'It would exceed my authority.'

Cameca explained that on the day of a perfect sacrifice the High Priests wanted as little attention as possible drawn to them on the streets. The warrior conceded that Tonila had ordered him to take a different route to the temple. Cameca held up the medallion.

'Autloc himself told me to give you this proof that I express his wishes.'

The warrior took it from her and studied both sides.

'It is the title to his dwelling and all his possessions,' he exclaimed.

'Who holds it, owns them,' Cameca hesitated and then

pointed at Ian. 'Well, until you deliver him to the temple.'

The warrior chuckled, went outside and sent the other two warriors off to watch the sacrifice. Ian gave Cameca a thumbs-up sign and had the impression that she understood.

'Mine until we reach the temple,' the warrior repeated, shaking his head in amusement as he came back inside. It was the last coherent thought he was to have for some considerable time, as Ian laid him out cold with a devastating chop on the base of his neck.

'I shall escort you to the temple,' Ian said. He went into the bedroom, took a warrior's half-mask and put it on his head. 'We overheard the route to take, didn't we, Susan,' he added as he came back to them.

Susan picked up the medallion. 'We must take this back to Autloc.'

'Leave it,' said Cameca, 'Autloc has gone.'

The Doctor had placed his pulley-wheel beside the strip of silk behind the curtain and made Barbara stand on the throne, her arms stretched up above her head with the coiled snake bracelet held between her hands. He made a few mental calculations.

'Exemplary, my dear,' he said. 'You may come down now.'

Barbara, with less than God-like grace, clambered off the throne, though in the final stages the Doctor did offer her his hand. 'As soon as Susan and Ian are here,' he said, 'you must insist that Autloc has them released.'

'Doctor, this temple will soon be lined with warriors and Tlotoxl will be present,' Barbara replied. 'Do you believe Autloc will be on our side?'

'I'm not a bad judge of character,' the Doctor said haughtily, 'and Autloc will do all he can to help us. I shall do the rest.'

'But your plan can't work,' Barbara protested, 'we won't escape. They'll stop us.'

The Doctor was aggrieved. 'My dear Miss Wright, the Aztecs will be preoccupied with their God, their human sacrifice, and an eclipse,' he said. 'What we do will be of no consequence to them.'

'I'll keep my fingers crossed,' Barbara replied without conviction.

They heard footsteps coming up the stairs.

'Hide!' said Barbara and the Doctor ducked behind the brocade curtain of the alcove.

Tlotoxl limped into the temple, a razor-sharp obsidian knife in his hand. Behind him came twenty warriors armed with javelins. Barbara watched them from the throne as they took up their positions along the walls. Tlotoxl sidled over to her.

'The procession has begun,' he snarled, 'the sacrifice awaits you.'

'Where is the High Priest of Knowledge?' Barbara asked.

'Gone,' Tlotoxl spat out the word.

'Where?' Barbara snapped back.

'Who knows?' Tlotoxl waved his arms. 'Into the wilderness, perhaps.'

'You have killed him.' Barbara's voice was cold, accusing.

Tlotoxl shook his head. 'No,' he hissed, 'you destroyed his faith in Huitzilipochtli. Autloc will never return.'

15

Eclipse

They made their way along the route Tonila had prescribed. The streets were deserted and the houses empty. As the Perfect Victim and Tonila mounted the stairs to the temple, the crowd moved to the square in front of the pyramid. Beyond an occasional 'Turn here' or 'That way,' the three of them did not speak, each of them absorbed in their own thoughts.

Ian knew that a final reckoning with Ixta was inevitable and, remembering all the warriors in the temple for the sacrifice to Tlaloc, realised he would be hopelessly outnumbered. But he also knew that Ixta would insist on single-handed combat, having made sure it would be a one-sided affair. Somehow, psychologically, he had to defeat Ixta.

Susan mentally had her fingers crossed and all her hopes were pinned on the possibility that her grandfather had dreamed up yet another near-miracle to see them out of trouble.

Cameca thought only of her beloved Doctor, whom she knew she would lose when she delivered Susan and Ian to the temple.

They came to the side of the pyramid and went towards the entrance where Ixta stood.

'I shall see us past,' Cameca said and when they reached Ixta she congratulated him on his appointment and added that she had been charged with delivering Susan to the temple. Ixta put his hand on Ian's shoulder.

'Where is Ian?' he asked.

'He follows with two other warriors,' Ian replied, disguising his voice as heavily as he could and pointing vaguely behind him.

'Escort them to the temple,' Ixta said.

The first victory, though a minor one, Ian thought as he followed Susan and Cameca up the stairs – nonetheless a victory.

The Perfect Victim and Tonila came into the temple. Tlotoxl, ignoring Barbara on the throne, led them ceremoniously out onto the terrace so that all the people in the square below could see them. The Perfect Victim spread out his arms as if to embrace them all. Tlotoxl drew Tonila to one side.

'First, as the sun is overshadowed, the handmaiden will be tortured and rendered blind,' he hissed, 'then Ixta will despatch Ian with his club and cast him off. And as total darkness comes I shall honour Huitzilipochtli with the perfect sacrifice. After which I shall deal with her,' Tlotoxl jerked his head back towards Barbara, then took Tonila by the arm. 'Autloc has gone,' he whispered, 'so you are now the High Priest of Knowledge.'

'I shall stand forever at your side,' Tonila replied with a bow.

Ixta waited for the two warriors to bring Ian, but they didn't appear and already the moon was edging its way in front of the sun. Suddenly, the truth dawned on him. The masked warrior who had taken Cameca and Susan to the temple was Ian. With a shout of rage, Ixta raced up the stairs.

Cameca and Susan entered the temple with Ian, who silently mouthed the words 'the Doctor' to Barbara. She glanced at the second brocade curtain. At least the four of them were in the temple, Ian thought, but so were the Perfect Victim, Tonila, Tlotoxl and twenty warriors with javelins. He turned to Cameca.

'For your own safety, go now, Cameca,' he said gently, 'and thank you.'

Cameca smiled bravely. 'Say farewell to the Doctor for me,' she said and he stepped from behind the curtain to take her hand in his.

'Goodbye, Cameca,' he said.

She touched his face with her hand and left the temple.

Tlotoxl stood on the terrace, looking up at the sun. A quarter was covered by the moon. Thorns lay on the altar.

'Seize the handmaiden so that she may be punished,' he ordered.

Two warriors grabbed Susan by her arms.

'Grandfather,' she called out.

The Doctor took a step towards her, but Ian stopped him with his hand as Barbara stood up.

'I, the Great Spirit of Yetaxa, forbid this punishment,' she commanded.

Tlotoxl limped into the temple from the terrace. 'You forbid it?' he snarled. 'Must I then order warriors to restrain you as you witness the thorns being thrust in and her eyes being gouged out?'

'I shall bring the thorns to you,' Ian said.

'Do so,' Tlotoxl replied, staring at Barbara.

Ian went to the altar and picked up the thorns one by one. Then he glanced up at the sun which was now one-third covered. Both Barbara and the Doctor wondered what Ian was up to.

'Make haste, the darkness descends,' Tlotoxl hissed.

'In obedience, High Priest,' Ian replied calmly, and threw the thorns over the parapet.

For an instant Tlotoxl gaped at the masked face. 'You!' he snarled. As Ian took off his mask, he turned to the warriors. 'Strike him down,' he ordered.

'No,' Ixta roared as he entered the temple. 'He is mine,' and he advanced menacingly towards Ian.

'I was worried it would be dark before you got here,' Ian said, backing round the sacrificial altar, making sure he kept it between himself and Ixta.

'Despatch him,' the High Priest of Sacrifice barked. 'The darkness comes.'

Susan, Barbara and the Doctor held their breath.

'Does it?' Ian asked as he took the biggest gamble of his life. He unclipped the pencil-torch from the inside of his loin-cloth and shone it on Ixta's face. 'Then let there be light.'

The Chosen Warrior's advance faltered. Ian flicked off the torch then put it back on again. Ixta's eyes dilated with fear as Ian aimed the beam of light at the cudgel and reflected rays bounced of the gold studs. With a horrified gasp, Ixta dropped it and Ian walked towards him flicking the torch on and off. Ixta backed away.

'The darkness comes, perfect sacrifice must be made,' Tlotoxl screamed so Ian shone the torch on the High Priest's face who cowered back against the wall. With the beam of light off him, Ixta made a dash along the parapet edge towards Ian.

'Chesterton!' the Doctor shouted his warning, and Ian swept the light back onto Ixta's face.

The Chosen Warrior checked himself, tried to turn

away, over-balanced and hurtled screaming to his death two hundred and fifty feet below.

'Now, Barbara,' the Doctor murmured. She pulled off the bracelet while the Doctor took his pulley-wheel and the silk strip from behind the curtain. Ian came in from the terrace shining the torch on the Aztec faces. When Tonila's was lit up, he sank babbling to his knees. Tlotoxl shielded his eyes but didn't move. Barbara threaded the bracelet through the hole in the middle of the pulley-wheel. The Doctor passed the silk over the groove and Barbara stood on the throne, holding the bracelet at arm's-length above her head. Susan ducked behin the brocaded curtain, gathered up the two bundles of clothes and dashed to the wall.

'Get your fingers under the wall as soon as you can, Susan,' the Doctor said as he tugged gently on the silk. The wall began to move.

'It's working, Grandfather,' Susan said as she dug her fingers under the base of the wall and helped to lift it up.

'Had to,' the Doctor replied, 'motion, dynamics, thrust. Everybody ready?' He didn't wait for an answer. 'Then off we go.'

Barbara clambered down from the throne, Susan grabbed their clothes, and with Ian last, still keeping the light shining on frightened faces, they went into Yetaxa's tomb pulling in the silk strip with them. The wall closed behind them as Tlotoxl scrambled to his feet.

'Sacrifice, sacrifice,' he screamed and two warriors went with him onto the terrace to lay out the Perfect Victim on the altar. Tlotoxl looked up at the dark sky, the sun now totally eclipsed, and raised the obsidian knife above his head.

'Huitzilipochtli, great God of the Sun,' he chanted, 'give us back your light as we, in your honour, make you perfect sacrifice.' He plunged the knife into the Perfect Victim's chest . . .

Inside the tomb everyone took a moment to catch their breath. Ian switched off the torch as the light from inside the TARDIS seemed sufficient. The Doctor took Yetaxa's bracelet from Barbara and began unthreading his pulley-wheel.

'Mustn't leave them something they haven't got,' he observed, 'it would confuse Cortez and his *conquistadores* no end.' He snagged the snake's head on the edge of the central hole. 'Chesterton, some light, please.' Ian pressed the button but nothing happened. 'Light, dear chap,' the Doctor insisted.

'Sorry, Doctor,' Ian replied, shaking the pencil-torch a couple of times, 'I think the battery's dead.'

Barbara ran her fingers around Yetaxa's mask. 'I failed, Doctor,' she said.

'It was inevitable, my dear,' he replied, overcoming the problem with the pulley-wheel.

'Then what's the point of us wandering through time and space?' she asked. 'We can't change anything. We're observers. Nothing more. Tlotoxl had already won the moment he first set eyes on us.'

'Yes, my dear,' the Doctor replied philosophically as he laid the bracelet on the slab beside the skeleton.

'And the one man I had respect for, I deceived,' Barbara said in self-accusation. 'I lied to Autloc, I gave him false hope and in the end he lost his faith.'

'The last time I spoke to him, he said he would pray to Quetzecoatl for us. Not Huitzilipochtli, my dear,' the Doctor replied. 'No, through you he found another faith, a better one. You couldn't save a civilisation, Barbara, but you helped one man.'

'I hope so,' she said and went into the TARDIS.

The Doctor put the pulley-wheel into his pocket and felt something else. He took it out and even in the dim light of the tomb he knew it was the brooch Cameca had given to him in the garden. It came from the tomb therefore it should be left in the tomb, he thought, but then again Cameca had given it to him as a present, so he slipped it back into his pocket, went into the TARDIS and closed the door.